a MAN

ANNE SCHRAFF

SADDLEBACK
EDUCATIONAL PUBLISHING

URBAN UNDERGROUND

A Boy Called Twister
The Fairest
If You Really Loved Me
Like a Broken Doll
One of Us
Outrunning the Darkness
The Quality of Mercy
Shadows of Guilt
To Be a Man
Wildflower

SADDLEBACK
EDUCATIONAL PUBLISHING
www.sdlback.com

© 2011 by Saddleback Educational Publishing

ISBN-13: 978-1-61651-008-4
ISBN-10: 1-61651-008-0
eBook: 978-1-60291-793-4

Printed in Guangzhou, China
0510/05-72-10

15 14 13 12 11   1 2 3 4 5

CHAPTER ONE

Trevor Jenkins let the door slam when he got home. Mickey Jenkins, his mother, yelled at him, "What you doin' comin' two hours late from school? What you been doin', boy?"

"Ma," Trevor groaned, his hands tensing into fists. He felt like punching a hole in the kitchen wall to let out some of his frustration. "I told you—we had track practice after school. Coach Curry is getting us ready for the meet against Lincoln." Trevor thought to himself that he couldn't take much more of this. Ma was worse than a warden at a maximum security lockup.

Mickey Jenkins came around the corner with the angry frown she always wore on her face. She was tall for a woman, a bit over six feet. She was all hard muscle, no fat. Her appearance brought to mind a tough length of leather. She worked as a nurse's aide in a rest home, and she could lift the patients, even men, with ease.

Trevor remembered being afraid of his mother all his life. It wasn't any better now that he was sixteen. But it hurt more, especially his pride.

"You never said it's gonna take you all of two hours, boy," his mother scolded. "Don't you be lyin' to me. I won't have that. I don't want you hanging around with your lowlife friends after school, you hear what I'm sayin'?"

She had raised her four sons without a husband. He had run off when the oldest was a little more than five and the youngest was a baby. She always swore she would raise her sons to be good, honorable men, even if she had to whup them every day, and she often did. Her eldest, Desmond, was now in the United States Army. A picture of him, a handsome young man proudly wearing his uniform, hung from the living room wall. He would soon be joined there by her second oldest, Junior, who was in boot camp. Tommy, who was a couple of years older than Trevor, was a freshman in City College. None of the Jenkins boys had ever gotten into trouble with the law, and Mickey Jenkins meant to keep it that way.

"I got no lowlife friends, Ma," Trevor protested. "I hang with Jaris and Derrick, and you've known those guys all my life. I grew up with them," Trevor dropped his school books on the floor. "You also know Kevin. He's a great guy."

"Don't be havin' no temper tantrums on me, boy," his mother said sharply. "You know well as me what I meant by lowlife friends. Jaris and Derrick and that Texas boy, Kevin, they're good kids. I got no problem with them. I'm talkin' about that hussy you been eyeballin' down at the yogurt shop."

Trevor stiffened. There *was* a pretty girl working at the Ice House, the new yogurt shop. Her name was Vanessa Allen, and she was beautiful. She had dyed dark red hair that looked beautiful with her cocoa-colored skin. Trevor never had had a girlfriend because his mother didn't believe in teenagers dating. Trevor had talked to Vanessa a few times and he liked her. She seemed to like him too. Vanessa had dropped out of Tubman High at the beginning of her sophomore year, and Ma considered all high school dropouts to be trash. "I don't know what you're talking about, Ma," Trevor lied.

"Y'know darn well what I'm talkin' about," Ma insisted. "Don't dummy up on me, boy. You gettin' hot and heavy with that trashy redhead works at the yogurt shop, that Allen girl. She's so bad she don't even live with her parents no more. She's only sixteen, and she's bad through and through."

"I'm not 'hot and heavy' with anybody, Ma," Trevor argued. "I went in a coupla times to get a frozen yogurt and she waited on me." Trevor wanted to scream. He loved his mother and he knew she loved him and his brothers. But she ran the house like a jailer, demanding to know where Trevor was every minute of the day. It had been the same with all the brothers, but the older ones had gone into the army, and she eased up on Tommy when he started college. Now she was able to give her full attention to Trevor.

"That no-good Allen girl," Mickey Jenkins ranted, "she lives with her trashy sister, and she can run wild there. Bad sorts comin' and goin' there all the time. I know what I'm talkin' about. I'm no fool, boy. Nobody pulls wool over my eyes. When your no-good Daddy walked out on us, I had four babies—four baby boys!—and I brought you all up by my own hard work. Army makin' men out of Desmond and Junior, but I still got work to do with you and Tommy, especially you, boy. You could go either way."

Trevor felt like the walls were closing in on him, threatening to squeeze him until he couldn't breathe. Anger was boiling up inside him. "Ma," Trevor pleaded, "I never been in trouble. I'm making good grades at Tubman. You can ask my teachers. I get along good with all of them. I never cause any hassles. Ma, can't you just get off my back for two minutes?"

Mickey Jenkins came closer to her tall, handsome son. "Boy, don't you talk to me in that tone of voice. I can still whup you up one side of your head and down the other, and you better believe it."

"I'm sorry, Ma," Trevor apologized, "but I just had a long track practice, and I'm tired. I need to do my homework, and you're screaming at me like I'm some criminal. Ma, you win! I mean, you got me whipped, okay? I don't even have the courage to buy a sandwich at school. I eat those hideous tuna fish sandwiches you make, those disgusting things. I eat them 'cause I'm scared of you."

"You remember the baggie, boy?" Ma asked, dragging out her most potent weapon.

"Oh man!" Trevor groaned, "I was like eleven years old, and I didn't even know what it was when the kid gave it to me to hold. You gonna throw that in my face again?"

"You were wild in those days, Trevor," Ma told him. "I had to be tough. Remember—I told you if I ever find a baggie on you again I'd kill you?"

"You gonna be throwing that at me when I'm an old man, Ma?" Trevor asked bitterly.

"I won't be around when you're an old man, boy," Ma declared. "I work sixteen hours a day for you and your brothers. The army is feeding Desmond and Junior right now, but I still got to see you and Tommy raised right. I don't ask for nothin' more than that. Every Sunday I go to the Holiness Awakening Church, and I ask God for nothin' more than to let my sons grow up good and decent men."

"I know, Ma," Trevor responded. "I'm doing my best."

"Okay," Ma said. "Just make sure you don't never lie to me about where you are. That's the beginning of trouble. When the kids start lying and tellin' stories. Next thing you know, the police are at the door telling you your child is in custody, or he's down at the hospital or the morgue 'cause he was drivin' drunk."

Trevor headed for his room. He felt like a steamroller had run over him. He grabbed his cell phone and called Jaris.

"Hey man, Ma is really on the warpath tonight," Trevor said.

Jaris was Trevor's closest friend. If you were Jaris's friend, he had your back. "Why?" Jaris asked, "What's going down, Trev?"

"I was late coming home from school 'cause of track practice," Trevor explained. "Coach Curry ran us longer than usual. She's like giving me the third degree, man. I don't know how much more of this stuff I can take. I'm coming in the door, and there's this fierce-looking woman who's my ma, and she looks like she's gonna take me down, man."

"Take it easy, dude," Jaris said. "Just hang in there. You'll be okay. Your mom probably had a bad day. She's got a rough job. Being tired makes some people mean."

"Easy for you to say, dude," Trevor replied. "You got nice, sane parents. You got a fun mom and a great dad. I think Ma is crazy sometimes."

"No, she's not crazy, man," Jaris told him. "She just loves you guys so much, and she's scared the streets will get you. They get a lot of guys. When your dad cut out, it made her hard and angry."

"Lousy bum!" Trevor said of his father. Trevor was a baby when his dad left, so he had no memories of his father. From time to time Trevor would see him on the street, often drunk, asking people for change for cigarettes or a bottle of wine.

"You still see your dad around?" Jaris asked.

"Yeah," Trevor answered. "I turn my head and look the other way. Just seeing him makes me sick. He doesn't try to talk to me. Not that I would want to talk to the old creep. He has a beard and he looks like he hasn't had a bath in a year. I'm telling you, Jaris, he played a dirty trick on Ma and us."

"There's too many men like that around," Jaris said.

"When he was with Ma," Trevor said, "he spent all his money on himself. Drinks, gambling. Then he quit his family altogether. Someday I'd like to just go up to him and ask him how he manages to sleep nights. I'd like to ask him if he ever thinks about us at all. But I'll never do that. I'm too much of a wimp. I'm so afraid of Ma I'm still eating those lousy tuna fish sandwiches at school."

"Trevor, your mom is probably so hard on you guys 'cause she's afraid you'll grow up like your father," Jaris suggested.

"Yeah, I know, Jaris," Trevor agreed, "but I'm making decent grades, and I'm good in track. I got nice friends. Why doesn't Ma come up to me and smile sometimes and say 'Good job, son'? Instead she's got that mad face on all the time."

"You're afraid of her and she's afraid of you, Trevor," Jaris said.

"Afraid of me?" Trevor asked incredulously. "I've never laid a hand on her. I wouldn't do that in a million years. She's beaten me up a lot, but I never ever thought of hitting back. I think hitting a woman is the lowest thing a man can do, but when she's your own mom—that's out of the ballpark, man. Means you're evil."

"No," Jaris explained, "she's not afraid you'll hit her. She's afraid you'll slip off track and go bad. That makes her mean and sour, dude."

"Jaris, I'm wondering, man, if you'd do me a big favor," Trevor asked. "I can't get through to my mom. But she's got a lot of respect for your mom. Would you ask your mom to find a way to talk to her? I just can't take much more. If your mom could, you know, just ask her to go out and eat for old times' sake or something. And then if she could just say something good about me. I know your mom likes me, Jaris. Your mom and mine both sing in the praise choir at Pastor Bromley's church. That counts a lot in my ma's book. She'd listen if your mom told her I was a good guy, and she didn't have to come down so hard, you know? Would you see if you could do that for me, man?"

"Sure, Trevor," Jaris agreed. "You bet. I'll tell my mom what's happening and she'll find a way to do it. She'll go to bat for you, man. Mom thinks you're a great guy."

Mickey Jenkins had only one day off during the week—Sunday. Monica Spain, Jaris's mother, invited her to go to breakfast after church.

"That'd be a nice change," Mickey Jenkins said. "That's real nice of you, Monica."

After church, Mrs. Spain drove Trevor's mother to a nice but inexpensive chain restaurant near the church. On the way to the restaurant, Jaris's mother asked, "How's everything going with your family, Mickey?"

"Oh, I can't complain too much," Mrs. Jenkins replied. "Desmond is a private first class in the army, and Junior is doing fine in basic training. Looks like he's gonna make it through. I don't worry much anymore about Tommy 'cause he's doin' good in college. Trevor, now that's the one I worry about. He's only sixteen. That's the worse age, you know, Monica."

"I've always thought Trevor was a really good boy," Mrs. Spain commented. "He and Jaris are the best of friends, you know. I've always been so grateful for that. Trevor has been a wonderful friend to my son, and I never worry when they're together."

"Oh Monica, that's real pleasing to hear," Mrs. Jenkins said. "But Trevor has a wild streak you know. Remember when I told you about him having that dope?"

"Mickey," Mrs. Spain protested, "that was ages ago. Trevor was just a little boy. He didn't even know what that stuff was. Jaris did worse at that age, I'll tell you. They do really stupid things in middle school. But now Trevor is a junior in high school. Jaris tells me the teachers really like him. And he's making good grades, isn't he?"

"Well . . . yes," Trevor's mother agreed.

They pulled into the restaurant parking lot, and Mrs. Spain said, "This is on me, Mickey. My treat. We don't get together to talk about our lives or our kids nearly often enough. There are no friends like old friends."

Mickey Jenkins smiled. She appreciated any chance she got to save a little money. Although she worked long hours doing hard, dirty work, she was paid poorly. The registered nurses earned a good salary, but Mickey Jenkins had never achieved that status. The nurse's aides were paid no more than the lowest clerical workers.

"My," Mrs. Jenkins remarked as they sat down, "this is such a nice place. When

I eat breakfast out, I'll grab something at a fast-food place, a burrito or something, and coffee."

"Order anything you like," Mrs. Spain urged her. "I love the French pancakes here. They serve them with strawberries and whipped cream. And then you get eggs and sausage too. I've even got coupons, Mickey. One breakfast is full price, but then the other is half price. So it's a real bargain."

"My goodness," Mickey Jenkins exclaimed, "French pancakes with strawberries and whipped cream. I feel like a queen or something. I never had much fancy food in my life. My mama raised us on grits with a little syrup."

When the waitress brought coffee, they ordered and waited for breakfast.

"I worry about Jaris too," Mrs. Spain started to say. "And Chelsea. She's fourteen and she's a little firecracker, Mickey. Sometimes Jaris gets into things over his head too, and then it's nail biting time for me. But I decided I would trust him. I know he's basically a good boy, just like Trevor. I used to bug him more, but now I don't. I would go, 'Why did you stay so long? Why didn't you call?'—all stuff like that. But I could see he was getting resentful. So I made up my mind I'd swallow my fears and trust my boy because he's a great kid, like Trevor is."

Mickey Jenkins looked thoughtful. "I ride Trevor pretty hard," she admitted.

"Well, we're mothers," Mrs. Spain said. "That's what we do sometimes, but we gotta just force ourselves to trust them. Now I give Jaris some space."

"You know, Monica," Mickey Jenkins replied, "thing with you is, you got a wonderful husband. Lorenzo, he's the best. He's such a good father for your children to look up to. My boys never had no father. I always felt guilty about that. I picked that bum. I picked Harry to be their father. I picked a man who deserted his wife and babies. Jaris can look up to Lorenzo and see what a good man is. But my poor boys . . . " her voice trailed off sadly.

"But Mickey," Mrs. Spain protested, "you've done a fabulous job raising those boys. Look at Desmond, a fine young man serving his country, and Junior on his way. Tommy and Trevor are both respectful and perfect gentlemen around our house. Don't underestimate the job you've already done, Mickey. You've raised three fine young men and Trevor is going to be number four."

"I sure do hope you're right, Monica," Mickey Jenkins said with a smile. "I do appreciate hearin' such nice things about my boys. I do so respect your family, Monica, and especially you. You have done a lot with your lives, you and Lorenzo, a nice home, your wonderful teaching career."

The waitress brought breakfast and Mrs. Jenkins' eyes grew huge. "Oh my goodness!" she cried. "Look at those straw-berries. That is so beautiful. And all that food. My goodness. This was so sweet of you, Monica. I'm not a very good cook, and we eat just plain food around our house. Oatmeal and toast for breakfast."

Monica laughed. "Oh, Mickey, I'm such a terrible cook that my kids pray their father will be cooking. Lorenzo is much better than me. I'm so busy teaching and marking papers that I usually don't even have time to cook at all. The kids have to put up with those frozen dinners. Bless their hearts, they don't complain, at least not to me. But I see those funny little peas and corn in the compartments, the rubbery looking chicken, and I think, 'What am I doing to my kids?'"

They laughed about their common lack of cooking skills and talked about the years past. Mrs. Jenkins remarked, "Monica, you were such a wonderful girl and now you're such a pretty woman. You're younger than me."

"I'm thirty-eight," Mrs. Spain announced.

"I'm forty-five," Mrs. Jenkins responded. "I remember I was already married to Harry when I'd see you walking by from high school, all the boys admiring you 'cause you were so pretty. I'd look at you and I'd think, 'She better pick a good boy to marry 'cause she's got a lot to choose from, that girl has.' "

Mrs. Spain replied, "I chose Lorenzo pretty fast. We met and fell in love in only a month!"

"Monica," Mrs. Jenkins went on, "I don't want you to be arguing with me on this. You have a good heart, a soft heart, and so you'll say to me, "No, no, it's not true,' but I know it to be true. I am gonna talk to you from my soul, Monica. I was as ugly as they come when I was a girl. I was six foot tall and just as plain as an old fence. Boys never gave me a second look. I wanted to fall in love and get married like all the other girls. I wanted to have children and a home. But nobody wanted me, Monica. Old Harry was the only one. I knew he was lazy and no good, but he the only one willin' to take me. I knew it was a big mistake, and he wouldn't be a good husband or a good father. But I went ahead anyway, Monica. I made this big mistake 'cause I wanted to have a husband and a family, and I never give it a thought what might happen with the children. And for that I feel sad."

"Mickey," Monica Spain responded, "don't you be calling it a big mistake. Never. I don't ever want to hear you say that again. How could bringing those four boys into this world be a big mistake? I've been to your house, Mickey, and I've seen photographs on the wall of Desmond in his uniform and Junior at camp, and all the boys in their gowns graduating middle school or high school. They're all such fine youngsters, Mickey. They're the best. No, that wasn't a mistake. Harry missed out and that's a tragedy, that's his bad. But you should be so proud."

A single tear gathered in the corner of Mickey Jenkins' right eye, and slid slowly down her face, a shiny bead of water on chocolate-colored skin. "Monica," she confided, "nobody has ever said words like you have said to me, and I will keep them in my heart like treasures."

"And ease up on Trevor," Mrs. Spain urged her. "Jaris tells me he's a light-hearted tease. He tries hard to be a good son, Mickey. Let him prove it to you."

CHAPTER TWO

On Sunday afternoon, Jaris, Trevor, and Derrick Shaw were going for a pizza. On their way they passed the Ice House, and a girl's voice sang out, "Trevor, we got some new flavors today. Want to sample them, you and your friends?"

"She sounds hot," Derrick said with a grin. "You *know* her, Trevor?"

Trevor grinned too. Having a pretty girl sing out his name was a new experience for him. "Oh," he replied, "I stopped here a couple times and got a yogurt, and we talked, just for a coupla minutes."

"She look as smokin' as she sounds?" Jaris asked.

Trevor shrugged. "She's kinda pretty, yeah."

"Maybe a yogurt would taste better than a pizza," Derrick suggested. "It's a pretty hot day for pizza."

"I'd like to see this chick," Jaris laughed.

The three boys went into the Ice House and a red-haired girl smiled at them. "You guys all look real familiar," she commented. "I used to go to Tubman High."

Jaris looked intently at the girl. "You look sorta familiar too. When did you go to Tubman?" he asked.

"I quit Tubman right at the beginning of my sophomore year," she answered. "I'm Vanessa Allen. I think I had a class with you, Mr. Pippin's English, but I don't remember your name."

"Jaris Spain," he said.

The boys ordered green mint frozen yogurt and sat at the counter.

"Why'd you drop out?" Derrick asked Vanessa.

"It got to be such a grind," she explained. "My mom and dad expected me to make good grades, but I hated all my classes. It was just so boring. I live with my sister, Dena, now. Dena's twenty and she likes having me around. I help her pay the apartment rent, you know. And we don't hassle each other. We're just free to do our own things. I mean, honestly, you guys, my parents never got off my case."

"I hear you," Trevor agreed.

Vanessa leaned on the counter where the boys sat. They were the only customers in the Ice House. Vanessa looked right at Trevor and told him, "You're so cute. I never had a class at Tubman with you. I would have remembered a guy as cute as you. I bet you got a girlfriend, huh?"

"No way," Trevor protested.

"Does that mean you don't *want* a girl-friend or . . . ?" Vanessa pressed.

Trevor shrugged. "I don't know," he said. He did know that Vanessa was very pretty and that he was attracted to her.

Trevor enjoyed looking at Vanessa even more than he enjoyed the frozen yogurt—and he *really* liked the icy yogurt.

Vanessa glanced at Derrick and Jaris. "I bet you guys have girlfriends, huh?" she inquired.

"Yeah," Jaris nodded. Derrick did too.

"What's wrong with your friend here?" Vanessa asked. She reached over the counter and walked her fingers up Trevor's cheek. "Hello baby," she giggled. "Want to play with me?"

Trevor smiled weakly and said nothing.

"Is he always this shy?" Vanessa asked the two other boys.

"Sometimes," Jaris said, "but give him time."

When the trio was out on the street again, Trevor remarked, "My ma already hates that girl in there."

"How come?" Jaris asked.

"'Cause she's a dropout," Trevor explained. "My mom thinks dropping out of school is a felony."

"Well, it's a stupid idea but it's not a crime," Jaris said.

"If I dropped out of high school, my parents would be crushed," Derrick added. "I could never do that."

"Vanessa sure is hot, Trevor," Jaris said. "And she's got her net out for you."

"Ma calls her a trashy redhead who lives with her trashy, no-good sister," Trevor replied. "And Ma says she's 'running wild,' whatever that is."

Jaris shrugged. "Seems like she's a pretty good worker at the Ice House. She must have some sense of responsibility."

Derrick split to visit Destini Fletcher, his girlfriend, and Jaris and Trevor were left alone. "Trevor," Jaris began, "I didn't want to talk about it in from of Derrick, 'cause it's just between us. My mom took your mom to breakfast this morning. They had a nice long talk."

Trevor's face lit up. "I haven't seen my mom today. Just a few minutes this morning before she left for church. Oh man, Jare, it would be so great if your mom got her to be a little less impossible."

"Well," Jaris responded, "when Mom came home this morning after breakfast, she said she really talked up what a good kid you were, Trev. She kind of came at it in a sneaky way. Mom is pretty sharp. She goes, 'Oh, we mothers worry a lot about our children and sometimes we're too hard on them. Like I worry about Jaris. Jaris is a big worry sometimes. I used to really nag him, but then he got upset, so I backed off. Besides, Jaris and Trevor are such good kids, they don't really need a heavy hand.' So Mom wasn't like criticizing your mom for how she's been. She was saying, you know, all moms worry too much, and they bug their kids and maybe they shouldn't."

"Oh man, dude," Trevor said. "I owe you for this."

"Let's hope it works, that's all," Jaris replied.

Trevor got home around noon. He told his mother that he'd been hanging with

Derrick and Jaris and that they'd all been doing their homework together. Even though Mrs. Jenkins liked Derrick and Jaris, she took a dim view of teens just hanging. Trevor always had to add some serious reason for his visits with friends, like schoolwork.

"Trevor?" Ma called out when the door slammed.

"Yeah Ma, I'm back," Trevor answered. He was about to spin another tale about him and Jaris and Derrick having made wonderful progress in preparing for Mr. Pippin's upcoming test. But before Trevor could say anything, Ma came around the corner without her usual angry frown. "Oh Trevor," she told him, "just the nicest thing happened this morning after church. I was going to just come home after services, but Monica Spain stopped me and invited me to breakfast. Jaris's mother just insisted I come along with her. I was just so surprised my jaw dropped, 'cause people don't do that out of a clear blue sky, but she's the nicest lady."

"Oh," Trevor replied, "that was nice."

"My goodness, boy," Trevor's mother went on, "she took me to this nice place, and we had the most beautiful, tastiest breakfast I've ever had in all my born days. French pancakes with strawberries and whipped cream, and then eggs and sausage too. I was so full I thought I'd not be able to eat another single bite for the rest of the day. And even better than the wonderful breakfast, we had the most pleasant talk. It just filled my heart, Trevor."

"Oh yeah?" Trevor said. "Well, she's nice. Jaris's mom is nice."

"She is that, Trevor," Mrs. Jenkins agreed. "And I think the best part of the whole morning was what she said about my boys. She just couldn't praise you enough, Trevor. She said she was so grateful Jaris had such a fine boy for a friend. Can you imagine what I felt when I heard that? That fine, high-quality woman who teaches school and lives in a pretty house, she's grateful that her son has the friendship of *my* son."

Trevor could hardly believe how a friendly smile instead of a frown on her face made such an improvement in his mother. With that angry frown she wore like a mask, she looked like an ogre. Now she just looked like a pleasant round-faced lady "Yeah?" Trevor asked.

To himself, Trevor thought, "Bless Jaris's heart. Bless his mother's heart."

"She went on and on about how the teachers at Tubman like you, boy," Mrs. Jenkins continued. "In my down times, I've bitterly regretted marrying your father, but Monica helped me to see it all in a brand new light. She put in my mind things I've never thought about. She said it was a blessing you four boys coming into the world, and I need not think I made a terrible mistake with your father. She said you and Tommy were perfect gentlemen."

"Wow!" Trevor said.

"You know," Mrs. Jenkins went on, "sometime I get so tired trying to care for those old people at the home. Many of them so cranky. They're sick. Who wants to be sick. They don't want to be there, and they take it out on the nurses and the aides. They fight with me a lot and I get cranky too, Trevor. I don't always mean what I say to you, boy. You know that, don't you?"

"Sure Ma," Trevor responded. He came over and kissed his mother's cheek. "I understand."

To himself Trevor said, 'Yesss!' "

At school on Monday, Jaris and his girlfriend, Sereeta Prince, met Derrick, Destini, and Trevor for lunch under the eucalyptus trees. Destini asked, "You guys get yogurt at the Ice House yet?"

"We did yesterday," Jaris replied. "It's great. And if you're short on money, you can buy one scoop."

"Talk about great," Derrick said with a wink, "Vanessa is hot."

Destini gave Derrick a mock shove. "You guys!" she declared. "You know what, Sereeta? We need to get blinders for our boyfriends. You know these flaps they put on the sides of horse's eyes? That's to keep the horse from seeing something that spooks them, but it would keep our guys from looking at other chicks."

Sereeta laughed. "Good idea. They could do it for husbands too."

"Guys never get over the urge to look at pretty girls," Trevor announced. "Ma tells me, where she works, guys in their eighties are still flirting with the cute nurses. When they hire a new nurse who's really hot, all the old guys perk right up."

Alonee Lennox came down the trail with Oliver Randall, her boyfriend, to join the others for lunch. "Trevor," she gasped, looking at his juicy hamburger with lettuce and tomato and onion on it. "You're eating a delicious looking sandwich, Trevor! What happened to those tuna fish deals your mom made you eat every day?"

Derrick smiled.

"This morning, like I couldn't believe it," he explained. "She goes, 'Hey Trevor, here's some money for lunch. You can get the kind of sandwich you like at school. We ain't so poor I can't handle that.' "

"The tuna fish sandwich was healthier for you," Oliver commented.

"Downer, man!" Trevor shot back, biting into his burger with gusto.

"We ought to stop at the Ice House and see who that hot girl is," Sereeta suggested. "As long as you think I can trust you, Jaris."

Jaris smiled. "You probably know her," he said. "Vanessa Allen. She was at Tubman during her freshmen year and for just a little of her sophomore year. She didn't dye her hair red then like she does now, but maybe you remember her."

"I remember her," Alonee recalled. "She was the biggest flirt in our freshman class. She'd come to school in these short, short skirts, and if our teacher was a cute guy, she'd try to sit up front right in front of him and flirt with him. You remember Mr. Collier? He was that young history teacher we had. He was like twenty-eight or something. She'd really go after him. He didn't know where to look anymore. Sereeta, you should remember her from the frozen yogurt shop."

"Oh my God!" Sereeta cried. "That was the same Vanessa? I never recognized her with the different hair color. We only worked the same hours one or two times. I remember her. She didn't like to study. She was flunking everything, and her parents were really giving her lots of trouble. She kept threatening to run away from home."

"Yeah, and she'd never want to go to the mall with us," Alonee added. "She said there weren't enough boys at the mall. I never remember her having a girlfriend, just guys."

Derrick said, "She's really got a thing for Trevor. You should see her eyeballing poor Trevor. You better watch out, Trev!" Everybody laughed.

Trevor finished his burger and grinned.

Tommy sometimes picked Trevor up from school in the afternoon, on his way home from the community college, but on Mondays, Trevor jogged home. He liked to jog and it strengthened his legs for the meets.

By taking a short detour on his way home, Trevor figured he could stop off at the Ice House. He thought he'd get a small scoop of frozen yogurt. He turned it over and over in his mind. He knew Ma would be angry if he did that, but how would she find out? She worked late on Mondays at the nursing home. She'd never know he stopped off for a green mint frozen yogurt and a few words with Vanessa. What was the harm?

"Why not?" Trevor asked himself, taking the detour. No girl had ever looked at him the way Vanessa did—at least not a girl who looked like her. That wonderful red hair really delighted him. He took the detour.

"Trevor!" Vanessa sang out when she saw him. "We've got a new flavor—mango peach. You can have a free taste. It's just come out and it's amazing."

"Okay," Trevor agreed. Vanessa handed him a little cup with the frozen yogurt and a tiny spoon. "Yeah, that's good," he said, finishing it. "I'll have a couple scoops of that."

Vanessa waited on several other students from Tubman. The Ice House was getting to be a popular place since the spring weather turned unseasonably warm. By the summer, business would be booming.

Then Vanessa came over to where Trevor sat. "Trevor, I get off work at six tonight. If you're ever bored or something, you could just come over here at six when my sister picks me up. She could pick you up too, and we could go somewhere for a little while," Vanessa suggested.

"Oh yeah?" Trevor said.

"Yeah, you don't even need to spend any money, Trevor," Vanessa told him. "We could watch a movie and eat popcorn at the apartment where I live with my sister. We could just hang there. It'd be fun."

"Yeah, I'll think about that," Trevor responded.

Vanessa reached out and ran her fingers down Trevor's arm, tickling him. "You're so sweet," she said to him. "I thought and thought, and finally I did remember you as a freshman. I wanted to be friends with you, but you said your mom was very strict and she didn't want you to go out with girls."

"Yeah," Trevor replied. He was ashamed to say, "She's still strict, and I'm still afraid of her." It was hard for Trevor to fully understand why he was so unwilling to break Ma's laws, unfair as they seemed to be. He thought of all the years growing up with her and of her working almost all the time at different nursing homes like a slave. She'd come home so tired she'd fall into the sofa and lay there gasping. And sometimes Trevor would get scared that his mother was dying, that she'd finally worked herself to death.

Trevor remembered feeling so sorry that his mother had to work that hard. He didn't know anybody else whose mother had to work so hard. Ma reminded Trevor of a poor draft mule, overworked and unappreciated.

Trevor's mother never had nice clothes. She had one decent flowered dress that she saved for Sundays. The rest of the week she wore T-shirts and dark trousers. She wasn't in the least bit heavy, and she even looked gaunt. She was muscular and tall, and to see her working, scrubbing, mopping, always working, you might think she was still enslaved. Trevor felt there was little difference between how his mother worked and how the slaves worked, and the thought made him sad and ashamed.

Trevor felt so sorry for her. It was so unfair what his father did, and yet Trevor couldn't do anything about it. He bitterly resented her iron rule, but he had a deep love for her. And he was unwilling to do anything against her rules, anything that would add to her burden.

Desmond and Junior had escaped into the army. Desmond once told Trevor that among his reasons for joining the army was to escape from Ma's rule. When he was in basic training, he told Trevor army life was easier than living at home. But Trevor didn't want to go into the army. He just wanted to finish high school, go to community college, and learn something that would get him a good job. Although he wanted to get away from his mother, he also wanted to be able to give her enough money so that she wouldn't have to work so hard.

"Baby," Vanessa commented, stroking Trevor's head. "You're so deep in thought."

Trevor was glad when four new customers came in, demanding Vanessa's attention. Still, he enjoyed seeing her bustling around. He wanted to take her up on her offer. He wanted to come over to the shop at six and then go to her place and have some fun.

Even though Ma had softened considerably since her breakfast with Jaris's mother, Trevor knew she would not approve of Trevor's going to Vanessa's place tonight—or ever. Ma was dead set against Vanessa Allen. Trevor knew the old angry frown would come back quickly if she learned that Trevor had been seeing Vanessa behind her back.

"But Ma won't find out," Trevor thought. If he played his cards right, he could have some fun with Vanessa and still not anger Ma.

Trevor worked part-time at the Chicken Shack, where Jaris worked almost every night. Trevor earned a few dollars, and he turned most of them over to his mother. He didn't begrudge her that help. He was just sorry he couldn't give her more.

But now the job at the Chicken Shack seemed to offer an answer to Trevor's dilemma. He didn't work on Monday night unless there was a sudden need, like another employee getting sick. Jaris worked Monday night, and all Trevor had to do was ask Jaris to cover for him in case Ma asked.

Trevor got more and more excited about tonight as he finished his mango peach yogurt. He smiled at Vanessa.

Her lips mouthed the words, "Are we on tonight, babe?"

Trevor nodded. He felt both excitement and fear. He took out his cell phone and called Jaris. "Hey man, you working at the Chicken Shack tonight, right?" Trevor asked.

"Yeah, why?" Jaris asked.

"Uh, I got a chance to hang with Vanessa for a couple hours," Trevor explained, "and I'm uh . . . telling Ma they need me at the Chicken Shack. You know, I don't like lying to Ma, but she'd never want me to be with Vanessa, but Vanessa's okay. So would you back me up if, you know, anybody asks?"

"Hey dude, I don't know if that's such a good idea," Jaris responded.

"We're brothers, right?" Trevor said, hanging up. He knew Jaris would get his back even if he didn't agree with what Trevor was doing. Jaris would never sell him out. He just wouldn't. Trevor knew Jaris well enough to know that. They always had each other's backs. It was a loyalty as deep as a blood bond.

CHAPTER THREE

Ma, I usually don't work at the Chicken Shack on Mondays, but tonight they're going to need me. I'll make a little extra money," Trevor told his mother when he got home.

"When you gettin' home, boy?" Ma asked.

"Uh, about eleven," Trevor replied.

"You want me to come pick you up? I'll be home by then," Ma offered. "My car is runnin' real good now."

"No Ma," Trevor declined, "the guy who manages the place can drop me home."

"You sure?" Ma asked, her brow furrowing with worry., "I don't want you runnin' around in the dark when all the no-goods are on the street."

"Honest Ma, I'll be fine," Trevor assured her. He wasn't feeling good about this, but he so wanted to be with Vanessa. He had never lied to his mother on any important issue, and he felt guilty. If his mother knew he was going to see Vanessa Allen, she would freak. Yet Trevor was doing it anyway. He was going against what she would want in a big way.

Trevor argued with himself furiously. One voice within him said, "Man, you're sixteen years old. You're a junior in high school. You shouldn't have to report to your mother about the girls you're going out with. It's none of her business. Dude! You're sixteen! You're almost a man. You *look* like a man. You're six feet tall. You drive a car when one's available. None of your friends have to confess every detail of their social lives to their parents. Even Jaris—good guy that he is—keeps secrets from his parents. He never shared with them some of his narrow escapes. Who does?"

But then he heard another voice. "Trevor, man, your mom has led a dog's life. She's got no life outside of working at that terrible job. She gets it from all sides. She's never had a vacation. She freaked out in gratitude when Mrs. Spain bought her breakfast. She's forty-five years old and some lousy pancakes are the highlight of her life. She owns one decent dress. All she wants out of life is to have good, obedient children who grow up to be good men. She doesn't like Vanessa Allen, and you should respect that. What kind of a girl drops out of school at sixteen and moves away from her family? Dropouts are people like B.J. Brady, who went from drug dealing to murder and ended up dying in a police chase. Dropouts are those kids with glazed looks hanging on street corners with no future. Why would any good kid want to date a high school dropout?'

Trevor didn't care. All he could think of was Vanessa's beautiful eyes and her wondrous red hair. He kept feeling her fingers on his arm—soft, like velvet. He tingled with excitement at the thought of her. No girl had ever made him feel that way before.

"Well, see you later, Ma," Trevor yelled as he went out the door. The Chicken Shack and the Ice House were both within easy walking distance of his home and in the same direction. As Trevor headed in that direction, it was still light and would be for another hour. Tonight, around eleven, Vanessa's sister would drive him home and nobody would be the wiser.

After all, Trevor thought, he wasn't doing something outrageous. Vanessa and he'd just watch a rented movie and eat popcorn. What was more innocent than that? Maybe he'd snuggle a little with Vanessa if she wanted to. No big deal. Jaris and Sereeta were always walking hand in hand and kissing each other under the eucalyptus trees.

It was a few minutes to six when Trevor arrived at the Ice House. Through the window he could see that the shop was pretty crowded, and there were a few kids from Tubman, but none that Trevor knew well. Ryann Kern and her parents were there, buying yogurt in a gallon carton. Ryann was a strange girl who had gotten into trouble at Tubman High by pretending she had money snatched from her purse. She didn't get along with most of the other kids. While Trevor was waiting, he spotted the big green Volvo that Sereeta's grandmother drove into the parking lot. When Sereeta and her grandmother came out of the shop, talking to one another, Trevor moved around the corner of the building to avoid being seen.

In the rear of the shop, Vanessa Allen had been changing from her Ice House T-shirt to street clothes. She appeared quickly in skinny jeans and a green turtleneck. Trevor felt his heart thumping again. Vanessa threw Trevor a big smile and sang out, "Let's go, babe." Her sister had just pulled up in a red Toyota with Beyoncé playing loudly on the radio.

"Dena," Vanessa said to her sister, "this is my friend, Trevor. We used to go to school together at Tubman, but we didn't know each other then."

"Hi Dena," Trevor said, getting in the car with Vanessa.

"Where to, Trevor?" Vanessa asked.

"Let's just hang at your place," Trevor suggested.

"Cool," Dena agreed. "Bo's there and he's making popcorn. He rented a great movie. It's supposed to be hilarious. Bo can really pick 'em."

Dena and Vanessa lived nearby in a small apartment. It was messy and crowded inside. Old beanbag chairs, some of them losing their beans, littered the floor in front of the television set, which was huge.

"This is Bo Wells, my boyfriend," Dena said to Trevor, nodding toward a tall, lanky man with a goatee. He looked at least thirty. He was filling bowls with popcorn.

"Hi Bo," Trevor greeted him. Trevor thought Bo looked a little spaced out, but maybe that was just him.

Everybody settled on the beanbags, and Dena turned on the movie. Vanessa was nibbling popcorn and sitting very close to Trevor, occasionally resting her red curls on his shoulder, something that suited Trevor just fine.

Trevor wasn't crazy about the movie—a chick flick. But just being there with Vanessa was good enough for him. The movie lasted about an hour and forty-five minutes, and then Bo went into the tiny kitchen and yelled to them in the living room, "Who wants some beer?"

"I do," Vanessa yelled back. Her sister added, "You *know* I do." Trevor replied, "Just cola or something if you got it."

Trevor didn't even want to imagine the consequences if he came home tonight with liquor on his breath. When Bo returned with the beer and Trevor's cola, he cast Trevor a wry smile and commented, "You don't get out much, do you, kid?"

"Well, I'm a junior at Tubman High, and I got a part-time job—" Trevor started to explain.

But Bo cut in. "I mean fun times."

Vanessa snuggled up to Trevor and remarked, "He's a very sweet boy. I've dated a lot of guys who drink and smoke, and I like Trevor better than them."

Trevor thought—she dated a lot of guys? She was only sixteen years old. "When did you start dating, Vanessa?" he asked her.

"I've been going on dates since I was thirteen," Vanessa replied, giggling. "My mom thought they were group dates, but we paired off quick."

Dena and Bo laughed. Trevor commented, "Thirteen's kind of young for a girl to be dating." Bo and Dena laughed louder.

"Remember that guy you dated last year?" Dena recalled. "What a creep he was. Gary-something? We called him 'scary

Gary.' He had a thing for you." Dena looked at Trevor and explained, "She met this loser on the Internet, and she couldn't get rid of him. He was all possessive and crazy-jealous. When Vanessa broke up with him, he'd park across the street *all day*. At night he'd shine his flashlight at our windows."

Vanessa started giggling again. "And then he'd throw pebbles at my window," she added. "All night, ping-ping!"

"Did you call the cops?" Trevor asked.

"I was going to, but then he stopped. I was so glad to be rid of him. He wasn't cute like you, Trevor," Vanessa said.

Dena and Bo were drinking a lot of beer. Then they switched to Red Bull and vodka. They were drinking from each other's glasses and laughing nonstop. Trevor looked at his watch. It was ten-thirty. The plan was that Dena would drive him home around eleven.

Vanessa noticed Trevor looking at his watch and said, "You got to get home, huh babe?"

"Yeah," Trevor answered.

Dena had been finishing her drink, and now she got up from the floor, almost toppling over. "Ewww, I'm a little tip-sy," she said with a slur.

"You're drunk, sis," Vanessa told her, shaking her head. "That girl is such a booze hound."

Trevor glanced at Bo. He didn't look too good either. "You guys," Trevor said, "I can jog home from here. It's only a couple miles farther than the Ice House and the Chicken Shack, and I always jog home from there."

"Oh Trevor," Vanessa objected. "I hate to see you having to go home in the dark."

"It's okay," Trevor assured her. "I'm on the track team at school and the more I jog, the better I get. I'm in the hundred meter at the next meet and I want to nail that."

"I'll drive you home, man," Bo offered. "I'm not drunk, just a little buzzed."

"No, thanks," Trevor declined. "I like to jog. I'll be home in no time. The days are getting hot now, so jogging at night when it's cool is a bonus."

At the door, Vanessa put her arms around Trevor's neck and said, "You're so nice. Do you think we can be friends? I so want to be your friend . . . "

"Yeah," Trevor said. Vanessa kissed him and he kissed her back. Trevor was surprised how easy kissing came to him. He was elated. Even if he had to jog home in the dark, he figured it had been a good night. Trevor felt he could not only run, but maybe even fly.

Trevor went out the door and looked in the direction he needed to go. He was about four miles from home. He knew his mother would freak big time if she knew he was going down these dark streets so late. The neighborhood gangs were more active at night.

But running this distance was no big deal for Trevor. He ran in some marathons for charity this year, and he was often in the top five. Going four miles at jogging speed was a breeze for him.

As Trevor ran, he thought he didn't like Vanessa's sister, and he totally did not like Bo. They were not the kind of people Trevor liked to hang with. He decided if he ever went on a real date with Vanessa, he'd take her out when Dena and Bo were not around. Trevor thought it wasn't Vanessa's fault that she had a creepy sister. That was just the way it was. Vanessa was there with Dena because she couldn't hack living at home anymore. Trevor could understand that.

Trevor fantasized sometimes about living somewhere else too—but where? If Tommy had a place, he'd bunk with him, but Tommy lived at home too. Trevor hoped Tommy would get a place of his own soon, and then Trevor could go with him. But that would have to wait until Trevor graduated from high school. Trevor liked his brother. He was a cool dude. He never pushed Trevor around, as big brothers sometimes do. Neither did Desmond or Junior. Trevor liked all his brothers.

Trevor was making good time when he noticed a car driving slowly alongside him. "Hey Trevor," Marko Lane shouted, "you escaping from somewhere, dude?"

"I'm just jogging, practicing for the meet," Trevor answered. Marko and Trevor were both good runners, and both were on the track team. One of them would probably win the 100-meter race against Lincoln. Kevin Walker and Matson Malloy were good too, but they weren't entered in the 100 meter.

"You heading home?" Marko asked.

"Yeah," Trevor admitted.

"Want a lift?" Marko offered. His girlfriend, Jasmine Benson, who was sitting beside him commented, "You look beat."

Trevor hesitated. He looked at his watch. Sometimes Ma got in earlier than eleven, and he wanted to be home before her so there wouldn't be questions. He hoped to get his shower in and look as though he'd been home for a while.

"Okay, thanks," Trevor accepted.

Jasmine opened the back door lock and Trevor climbed in. "Heyyy," Jasmine noted when she got a good look at him. "You got lipstick all over your face, Trevor Jenkins. What you been doin' boy? Did a rabbit wearing lipstick jump out from the bushes while you were jogging and kiss you? And why are you in your street clothes?"

Marko was driving the car, but he turned and glanced back at Trevor, who was frantically wiping his face. "You been leading a secret life, dude?" Marko asked.

"I was out jogging and I met somebody," Trevor explained, sorry that he'd accepted the offer of a ride.

"Man," Marko taunted, "you are one hot dude. You're jogging in the middle of nowhere and along comes a babe to lay her kisses on you."

Jasmine laughed. "Trevor's the quiet one, but that's the kind you gotta watch out for!"

"Who's the babe, dude?" Marko asked. "Somebody from school?"

"No, just a girl from the neighborhood," Trevor answered. He felt miserable. Why was he so stupid that he didn't wipe off Vanessa's lipstick?

"Your mama wouldn't be happy if she knew strange babes were laying kisses on you, dude," Marko told him.

"His mama," Jasmine added, "she is something else. She is big and tall, and she'd scare the devil if he ever showed up at her door. I never saw such a fierce lady. You better watch out, Trevor. Your mama finds out you been hanging with babes behind her back, she gonna break you in two like a matchstick!"

"I'm glad my mom isn't like that," Marko commented. "She trusts me. She's a businesswoman, and she's so busy making money she got no time to bird-dog me."

Marko pulled into the driveway leading to the Jenkins' house. It was a two-bedroom frame house that Mrs. Jenkins rented. At one time Ma slept in the living room on the couch, and the boys shared the bedrooms.

Now Ma had a bedroom and Tommy and Trevor shared the other one with a curtain between them for privacy.

"Thanks for the ride, Marko," Trevor said, jumping eagerly out of the car. Ma hadn't arrived home yet.

"Sweet dreams, dude," Marko yelled from the window. Jasmine laughed hysterically.

Trevor rushed into the house to find Tommy doing homework on his laptop. He had a pretty good part-time job now at an electronics store, and he got the laptop cheap. He looked at Trevor as he came in. "Ma said you had to work at the Chicken Shack tonight," he mentioned.

Trevor trusted his brother not to rat him out. He had to talk to somebody and Tommy was a good guy. "I told her that, but I had a date," Trevor admitted. "I knew she wouldn't like that, so I lied."

"You got a girlfriend?" Tommy asked.

"Sort of," Trevor said. "She works at the Ice House and she really likes me. Ma hates her 'cause she's a high school dropout, but I can't shut it down, Tommy. I like this girl a lot."

"That'd be the redhead, Vanessa Allen, right?" Tommy guessed. "I've seen her at the Ice House. She was a freshman at Tubman when I was a junior. She's bad news, bro."

Trevor stiffened. "What're you talking about?" he asked. He didn't expect Tommy's opposition too.

"She just is, man," Tommy stated flatly. "You shouldn't be hanging with her. She made a lot of trouble at Tubman. She got a teacher fired."

"How did she do that? A little sophomore girl," Trevor argued.

Tommy told Trevor the story. "She flirted with the guy and when he wouldn't take her bait, she went to the vice principal and told lies. I'm telling you, Trev, you're playing with fire."

Trevor stood there staring at his brother. "You won't rat me out to Ma, will you?"

Tommy's reaction frightened him. Tommy seemed to hate Vanessa Allen as much as Trevor's mother did. Trevor was shocked. His brother's advice was totally unexpected. He thought Tommy would help him in his budding social life.

Tommy looked Trevor straight in the eye and said, "You think I'd tell Ma you lied about working tonight and instead you hung out with a cheap little chick?"

"No," Trevor said in a faltering voice. "I don't think you would."

"You'd be right," Tommy assured him.

Trevor didn't believe the story his brother told him about Vanessa. He didn't think Tommy deliberately lied, but gossip has a way of starting small and getting out of control. Vanessa was too nice a girl to have done something like that. Or so Trevor believed.

CHAPTER FOUR

Trevor took his shower and tidied up the house for his mother. She'd be pleased that he had done that. When Trevor's mother came in, he greeted her. "Hi Ma. Everything okay at work?"

"As okay as it always is," Ma sighed wearily. She collapsed into one of her easy chairs, as she always did when she got home from a long day. "Patients grumpy, work never ends. The usual. I'm used to it. But that's why I'm always houndin' you boys to finish school and be able to get a good job. Desmond, he's in the army now, and he's just not learnin' to be a good soldier. He's learnin' a lot of technical stuff that's gonna help him when he leaves the army.

Those boys come outta the military with good skills. They won' end up like me, workin' like a slave for chump change." Ma looked up then. "You get home okay from the Chicken Shack? I was worryin' about you, boy."

"Yeah Ma, fine," Trevor assured her, the lie bothering him again. He glanced at Tommy standing over in the corner. Tommy gave him a look, but he didn't say anything.

"See," Ma continued, "that work at the chicken place, that's okay for a boy. But a man, he needs more. Imagine you droppin' out of school and ending up at the Chicken Shack when you're thirty years old. Like your father. He didn' have the gumption to finish high school, so he just done dropped out. Got a job in a car wash. Then cleanin' up the pool hall. Now he's forty-seven years old and he's stumbling around the streets lookin' for strangers to give him change for a cup of coffee." Ma got up heavily, shaking her head. Her legs were bothering her. Her back was bothering her.

Years ago, she'd told Trevor that all nurses end up with bad backs from lifting patients. After she couldn't work anymore, she'd be an old lady with a bad back.

Trevor couldn't sleep well that night. He worried about Marko and Jasmine seeing him late at night with lipstick on his face. Marko was the kind of a guy who might use information like that against Trevor if he wanted or needed to.

On the way to school the next day, Trevor dreaded having to look at Jaris after he asked his friend to lie about working at the Chicken Shack. Trevor decided he'd try to avoid Jaris and eat his hamburger on a grassy knoll at the other side of the campus.

But Jaris caught up with Trevor on the way to Mr. Pippin's English class. "Did you get done whatever you needed to do last night, Trevor?" Jaris asked.

"Yeah, I did," Trevor answered.

"Who is she?" Jaris shot back.

"What are you talking about, man?" Trevor asked.

"Dude," Jaris snapped, "Marko Lane and Jasmine just told me you had a hot date last night and they gave you a ride home. You had lipstick all over your face. It's none of my business, Trevor. But if somebody asks me if you were working at the Chicken Shack last night, I'm expected to lie for you, and I don't like that. And you know Marko's going to have it all over school before lunchtime. When a lot of kids know you weren't at the Shack and I say you were, then I look like a liar and a fool, okay?"

"Jaris," Trevor whined, "you know how Ma is. There's this girl who likes me and Ma hates her. I've never had a girl like me this way. You gotta understand, man. What am I gonna do? Sure, my ma's been nicer to me since your mom took her to breakfast, but she still wouldn't want me dating Vanessa."

"Well, just watch yourself, dude. Don't get in over your head, you hear what I'm saying?" Jaris advised.

"Jaris," Trevor replied, "we just went to her place and we watched a dumb movie and ate popcorn. It's the kind of harmless thing anybody'd do. But I was with Vanessa and that meant a lot to me."

As they approached Mr. Pippin's classroom, Marko and Jasmine were already there at the door.

"Here comes lover boy," Marko announced.

Jasmine blew Trevor kisses. "Here you go, honey. Mine don't even leave marks."

"Knock it off, you guys, please," Trevor said.

"Trevor's got a secret love," Jasmine giggled. "He meets her by the light of the moon."

Mr. Pippin came along, lugging his old briefcase. Mr. Pippin and the briefcase seemed to be aging together. Each day Mr. Pippin had more wrinkles and the briefcase had more cracks in it.

"Today," Mr. Pippin announced, "we are examining the nature of reality. We will base our discussion on the story you all have presumably read, Plato's 'Allegory of the Cave.'"

Marko raised his hand. "I didn't understand that story, Mr. Pippin. All those guys in the cave looking at the shadows on the wall. What were they doing there? Were they criminals? I mean, I didn't get it."

Mr. Pippin frowned. "Marko," he explained, "that isn't the point. The point is that the people in the cave thought that those shadows were everything. They did not know there was a larger world out there beyond the cave. What they saw as reality was just a small part of the world."

"I just don't get it," Marko insisted. "That guy Plato didn't explain things good. Who was he anyway?"

"Some old Greek," Jasmine said.

"Maybe there's another way to talk about reality," Oliver suggested. "Let's say you saw a bunch of people running down the street. They're sweating and straining. You're thinking—what's this? A riot? Are they chasing somebody? There's a guy out front, and they seem to all be chasing him. What are they going to do to him when they catch him? What's this guy done anyway to get all those people chasing after him? But what are we really looking at?"

Derrick raised his hand. "There's been an earthquake, and everybody's running from it, and the guy up front is leading them to a safer place."

Some students snickered, and Derrick Shaw's friends just smiled. Derrick usually gave the wrong answer.

Mr. Pippin looked delighted. Once again Oliver Randall had gone beyond his expectations. Randall's father was an astronomy professor who knew Mr. Pippin at UCLA. Whenever Mr. Pippin had almost completely lost hope in his students, Oliver came up with something. "Yes," Mr. Pippin responded, "what is truly happening here? What is the reality of this situation?"

Jasmine raised her hand and said, "Looks like they've all gone crazy. Like mass hysteria."

"No, no," Oliver replied. "It's a marathon. They're all running a race."

"Yes!" Mr. Pippin cried. "So simple. The man in front is the fastest and they're out to pass him."

"Man," Marko Lane complained after class, "that jerk Randall is a showoff."

Jaris and Trevor walked together to their next class. Trevor was still trying to explain himself to Jaris. "Vanessa's a nice girl. Sure, she did a dumb thing dropping out of Tubman, but that's no reason for Ma to hate her."

"Well Trevor, I don't know the girl," Jaris replied, "but Marko and Jasmine are spreading the word about your hot babe. Sooner or later it's gonna get back to your mom, and she's gonna go ballistic. If I were you, I'd tell her before she hears it from somebody else."

"Man, you don't know what you're asking me to do," Trevor said with a shudder.

"Maybe you should just drop the girl, Trevor. How long have you known her?

You can't be that connected already," Jaris suggested.

"I can't do that, Jaris," Trevor told him, "you've always had girls interested in you. Now you got Sereeta and she's the best. But I never could get involved with a girl 'cause of Ma. Now a really cute, nice girl likes me, and I'm not giving her up. I never knew having a girlfriend could make you feel so good, man. I like the feeling. If I gotta live this way, I will. If I have to be afraid of Ma and deny myself friends like you got, like Kevin and Oliver and Derrick got, I will. Maybe I should just load my stuff in a garbage bag and hit the road."

"Don't do that, man," Jaris advised. "Your mom's coming around. She's gonna change. It's too bad Vanessa doesn't go to school at Tubman, and your mom could get to meet her parents at school things. That would go a long way to putting her mind at rest. But Vanessa is estranged from her parents, right?"

"She told me her parents were on her case all the time," Trevor explained. "She couldn't take it. I can feel for her. It's like you're in prison, but you never did the crime."

"I wonder if her parents still live around here. Maybe you could talk to them," Jaris suggested.

"No, I'd never do that," Trevor objected. "It would be like checking up on Vanessa. I know what I'd feel like if she called Ma. She got away from her parents because they were impossible, just like Ma is."

After school, Jaris and Trevor were standing near Harriet Tubman's statue when Tommy Jenkins drove up to take Trevor home.

Before Tommy got close, Jaris asked, "Does your brother know you're dating Vanessa?"

"Yeah, but he's not on my side," Trevor admitted.

"What's that supposed to mean?" Jaris demanded. "Your brother has *always* been on your side, dude. All you Jenkins boys have stuck together every time. I always admired that. Tommy's rock solid."

"He's against Vanessa too," Trevor insisted. "He told me some crazy story about how she got a teacher fired at Tubman when she was a sophomore."

Tommy came walking over to where Jaris and Trevor stood. Tommy looked at Jaris and asked coldly, "Jaris, do you know who this fool is dating?"

"Yeah," Jaris admitted, "but I don't know much about the girl. I vaguely remember her as a freshman."

"Yeah, well she's trouble," Tommy asserted bitterly. "She lied about a teacher and got him fired!"

"What teacher?" Jaris asked.

"You remember Mr. Collier?" Tommy replied.

"Oh yeah. That young guy," Jaris recalled. "He was almost as shy as the students. He was nice though. Good looking dude. Some of the girls had crushes on him."

"Well, I was a junior then and we found out what happened," Tommy explained. "Vanessa flirted with that teacher every chance she got. When he put her in her place and demanded she quit doing that, she got even. She went to see that wimp of a vice principal we got, Mr. Hawthorne, and told him Mr. Collier was harassing her and trying to make dates with her. Hawthorne has no backbone, so he went the easy way. Mr. Collier wasn't asked back for the next school year. Hawthorne figured it was a scam, but he was terrified of the publicity. Poor Collier didn't have tenure, so it was easy to let him go. Hawthorne used some lame excuse that Collier's discipline was weak. But it was her. It was Vanessa Allen who got him out."

"I don't believe that," Trevor insisted. "Vanessa's too nice to have done something like that."

Tommy looked at Jaris and rolled his eyes. "My little brother is stupid, Jaris. He's gone stupid on us."

Trevor got in Tommy's car, and they headed home.

"We gotta clean up the house a little, maybe mop the kitchen floor," Tommy said. "Ma was really tired when she left for work this morning. She was moaning about the dirty kitchen floor, so we gotta take care of that."

"Sure," Trevor agreed. "I'll do that." Trevor looked at his brother as he was driving home. "Tommy, when you were at Tubman, didn't it bother you that Ma didn't want you to date? You're a lot cooler than I am, so a lotta girls must have been looking in your direction. I mean, how'd you handle it?"

"Yeah, it bothered me," Tommy confessed. "But I thought to myself when I'm in the community college it's all gonna be different. I'll make up for lost time. I got a girlfriend now, Trevor. She's great. She's planning to do something good with her life just like I am. She looks like a keeper, man."

"But that seems so long to wait," Trevor objected.

"Two lousy years when you're starting your junior year. One year when you're finishing it like you are. Trust me, Trev, it's worth the wait," Tommy advised. "Hey, little brother, I hear you. I know. I know it's not right what Ma is doing. She's impossible a lot of the time. But, you know, she provides a roof over our heads. Imagine what it was like for her when the old man cut out. We were all little and it was all on her. Uneducated, no money to speak of, four hungry babies yelling for food. Yeah, she went a little crazy, but Trev, she's earned the right to be a little nuts."

"Remember how she'd whup us, Tommy?" Trevor recalled. "I remember being like ten years old, and she'd whup my backside so hard I couldn't sit down right for days."

"Yeah, mine too," Tommy recollected. "But look around the neighborhood. How many guys from here in jail, in the cemetery? I don't know what I'd be like if she hadn't bullied me. I remember hanging with a couple of guys from the Nite Ryders when I was fourteen. I thought they were really cool. Ma caught me, and dragged me in the house, and knotted a wet towel, and hit me again and again. If somebody had seen her, maybe she'd of gotten in trouble and us kids would've ended up in foster care. Who knows? But I know one thing. I never hung with those Nite Ryders no more."

"But Tommy," Trevor protested, "our friends are doing okay, and they're not catching it from their parents like we did from Ma. Look at a guy like Jaris. Nobody leaning on him like that and he's fine."

"You know what, Trevor?" Tommy asked, "I got a story to tell you. I didn't hear it from Jaris. He never would've told. I heard it from another guy who was there that night. It's about Jaris's sister, little fourteen-year-old Chelsea. A while back she started hanging with this freshman from Tubman, a guy named Brandon Yates. She was going to his house for a party, and she lied to her parents. She said she was going to study with a girlfriend, but she was headed to this party. She gets there and they're all smoking dope and drinking.

One of the guys there was that drug dealer, B.J. Brady, the guy who ended up murdering another guy and being killed in a police chase. Just think about it. There was this innocent little fourteen-year-old in there, and who knows what might've happened. Except Jaris saw her sneak off, and he dragged her out of there, and told Yates he'd bust his head if he ever came near Chelsea again. You see what coulda happened? The Spains, they're great people, but Chelsea wasn't afraid to lie and almost got herself in deep trouble. They're nice, not tough like Ma. So Chelsea wasn't afraid to lie and put herself in danger. She knows sweet Mrs. Spain isn't going to whup her with a knotted wet towel, like our ma. So who knows what's right and what's wrong? I know this, Trevor, our mom loves us so much she would die before seeing us go bad, and there's something to be said for a love like that, dude."

Trevor felt sad and frightened. He was afraid his mother would find out he had lied.

He was ashamed that he'd gone against her rules, even though he thought they were wrong.

Still, deep down in Trevor's heart, he knew he would not—could not—give up Vanessa Allen. He kept seeing that pair of smoky eyes, the red lips, the wonderful red hair around her soft face. He kept feeling her fingers on his skin. He wanted to see her again. He would see her again. He was sure of that.

CHAPTER FIVE

When the boys got home, Trevor mopped the kitchen floor and dusted around the living room where Ma kept her few treasured possessions. She had a glass figurine of an angel that was a gift from her mother, long dead. Trevor didn't know if it was worth anything, but it was beautiful, and he dusted carefully around it. Alongside the glass angel was a clown figurine. Trevor never knew who gave his mother the clown, but she was attached to it. The clown had a sad face, with tears painted on his cheeks. Trevor dusted the clown too.

Trevor did his homework and went to bed. After tossing for about an hour, he finally fell asleep. Then the nightmare came.

In the nightmare, Trevor was lying in bed, and his mother came into the room. She carried in her hand a huge wet bath towel, the biggest one Trevor had ever seen. Several knots were tied at the end of it.

"Trevor Jenkins!" Ma shouted. "You lied to me about working at the Chicken Shack." The wet towel came crashing down over Trevor's face. "You were with that trashy redhead, Vanessa Allen." Again the knotted towel crashed against Trevor's face. The beating went on and on, and Trevor thought he was going to die. Ma was finally going to kill him.

Trevor woke up shaking, his face throbbing. He imagined it red and bruised, perhaps bloody. He got out of bed, staggered into the bathroom, and turned on the light over the mirror. He stared at his undamaged face. He hung his head over the basin for a moment until he stopped trembling.

Trevor turned slowly and walked down the hall to his mother's room. She lay across the bed in her old faded nightgown.

She had not even bothered to pull the blankets up over herself. She had apparently been so tired she washed up, got into her nightgown, and fell across the bed with all the blankets gathered at the bottom of the it. It was chilly in the house because Ma kept the thermostat down to conserve on the energy bills. She lay there and she was cold. Trevor carefully pulled the blankets up from the bottom of the bed and covered her. She didn't wake up. She was sleeping too soundly. Hers was the deep sleep of exhaustion.

When Trevor went back to his room, he called Vanessa. "Hi," he said quietly into the phone. "Did I wake you?"

"No Trevor, how's it goin'?" Vanessa asked.

"I was just thinking about you, Vanessa," Trevor replied.

"I think about you all the time, babe," Vanessa told him. "I'm sorry about the other night that you had to walk home. I didn't think my dumb sister would drink so much. I thought maybe you were mad at me about that. I felt so bad."

"Oh no, I wasn't mad," Trevor said. "I like to jog. It helps me run faster on the track team. You sure I didn't wake you up? It's almost eleven thirty. You must think I'm crazy calling you at this hour, huh?"

"Babe, I was watching a movie," she explained. "It just ended a couple minutes ago. I watch old movies when I get home from work. I love old movies. I like old actors and actresses like Humphrey Bogart and Ingrid Bergman. I've seen *Casablanca* a zillion times."

"You get off work tomorrow at six?" Trevor asked.

"Yeah," she said.

"Maybe we could hang out, you know? I can borrow my brother's car 'cause he gets home early tomorrow. We could just go watch the sun go down in the bay. No big deal. Just an hour and a half or something," Trevor suggested.

"Oh, I'd love that!" Vanessa exclaimed.

"Okay, six tomorrow. See you, babe," Trevor signed off.

When Tommy was leaving for community college in the morning, Trevor went to his car. "Give me a lift to Tubman?"

"Sure, why not," Tommy agreed.

"Tommy," Trevor said when they were on the way, "when you get home from school tomorrow, can I borrow your car for just a couple hours? Like maybe six to eight-thirty or something like that?"

"What for?" Tommy asked.

"Man, I know all you told me, but I want to see her," Trevor confessed. "We're just going down to the bay to watch the sun go down. Tommy, maybe what you said is true and she did a bad thing, but that was two years ago, and she's real sweet now. You can't hold something against a person forever. I really need your wheels, man."

"Okay, fool," Tommy said. "On one condition. If this thing blows up, don't tell Ma I loaned you my car so you could go see Vanessa. I don't want Ma coming down on me. You tell her I loaned you the car to do stuff with Jaris. Deal?"

"Yeah, you bet," Trevor agreed. "It's all on me, man. Thanks a million."

"Don't thank me, sucka," Tommy warned him. "I'm helping you get in trouble. I'm doing what they call 'enabling.' I'm making it easier for you to get mixed up with a loser."

At lunch at Tubman High the next day, Trevor ate under the eucalyptus trees with his usual circle of friends. Jaris Spain and his girlfriend, Sereeta, were there, along with Oliver, Alonee, and Sami Archer. Sami's boyfriend, Matson Malloy, was busy practicing for the track meet coming up against Lincoln. Sami had just been crowned Princess of the Fair at the Tubman High Medieval Fair. Everybody had expected the honor would go to a beautiful girl like Sereeta Prince, but Sami was popular with everyone for her good heart and willingness to help. She was overweight, but what most people noticed about her were her bright dancing eyes and a smile that wouldn't quit. The Princess of the Fair title was intended to go to the girl who best exemplified the courage and compassion of Harriet Tubman, the school namesake. That was Sami.

"So," Sami declared. "Everybody buzzing about you having a girlfriend, Trevor. Old Marko and Jasmine talking it up that you had lipstick on your face the other night after a hot date."

"That fool can't keep his nose out of other people's business," Oliver commented. Oliver had already had his problems with Marko. Once he almost punched him out.

Trevor looked down for a moment, then he responded. "Ma doesn't want me having a girlfriend, you guys. Oliver, you're new around here, so you don't know my ma. She's one tough lady. She's worked hard and sacrificed for me and my brothers, but she's like a prison warden. She watches me like a hawk. She doesn't like the girl I'm hanging with, so I gotta see Vanessa in secret."

"Who's Vanessa?" Oliver asked. "Does she go to school here?"

"Vanessa Allen," Trevor replied. "She's sixteen, but she dropped out of Tubman in tenth grade. Ma thinks dropouts are trash. But Vanessa is really a nice girl, and she likes me a lot. I mean, you guys, don't I have a right to have a girlfriend? You guys all have girlfriends. Your parents aren't throwing fits over that."

"Nothin' wrong with having a girlfriend, dude," Sami noted. "Your mama just worried that when you hang out with dropouts, sometime you drop out too. You think, 'Hey, she dropped school an' she's doin' fine. So why am I goin' through all this stuff?'"

"Sami, I'm gonna finish Tubman," Trevor told her, "and then I'm going to community college like Tommy. I'd never drop out. I've always worked hard to get good grades, and now I got a B average, and I'm on the track team and getting better all the time. Coach Curry said I could get an athletic scholarship if I keep going like I am."

Jaris knew the story about Vanessa's getting Mr. Collier in trouble. He'd heard it from Tommy Jenkins, but he wasn't going to say anything about it to those of his friends who didn't know. Jaris didn't know if the story was true, but he wasn't going to spread it. If Trevor wanted the gang to know, he'd have to tell it.

"What does Vanessa do now that she dropped out?" Sami asked.

"She works at the Ice House," Trevor answered. "She works almost every day. She lives with her sister and she pays her way. She's not some wild, crazy kid like Ma thinks."

"Has your mom ever met Vanessa?" Oliver asked.

"Are you kidding?" Trevor said with a shudder. "If I brought the girl home, Ma would chase her out with the broom!"

Jaris said nothing. Alonee turned to Jaris and asked, "You've met her, haven't you? At the Ice House? What did you think of her?"

Jaris shrugged. "I don't know. I just said a few words to her. She seemed okay. You can't find out much about somebody in a few minutes eating yogurt."

"You guys," Trevor groaned. "I don't know what to do. I don't want to make Ma mad, but I can't give up Vanessa. I'm not in love with her or anything, but she's so fun to be around and I think of her an awful lot."

"You know what, Trevor?" Sami advised. "I got a plan. Lissen up, boy. My mama knows your mama. I'll ask my mama to invite your mama to the Ice House for some frozen yogurt some afternoon. When that girl Vanessa comes to serve them, she gonna be real nice and ladylike. You gonna prime the pump, boy. You gonna tell Vanessa to be extra nice when the ladies come in. My mama'll say something like, 'Well, hello Vanessa. All the kids been talking 'bout what a good server you are. You sure seem hard-working. Understand you dropped out of Tubman, but you going for your GED pretty soon I'll bet!'"

Trevor smiled broadly. "Wow Sami!" he exclaimed. "That sounds great!"

"Yeah," Sami said. "You tell Vanessa to say she's sorry she quit Tubman, and she wants that GED. So then maybe your mom won't be so hard on her. She'll see her in a whole different light."

"I'm going to see Vanessa today around six," Trevor said. "We're just taking a little drive to watch the sun go down on the bay. I'll tell her your mom and mine'll be coming into the Ice House. Oh Sami, you're wonderful! No wonder they elected you Princess of the Fair! When Ma really meets Vanessa, she won't think of her as some sassy little witch anymore. When Ma sees that pretty chick being all sweet and polite, she's bound to soften up."

"Well," Sami said, conspiratorially, "your mom gets off work at the Maples Convalescent Home around noon on Wednesdays. I know 'cause she and my mom do their wash at the little laundry across the street. Your mom don't go back to work till three. So it'd be sometime after noon and before three that Vanessa should be expectin' two ladies in the prime of their lives. Mom is forty-one, and she all the time sayin' she in the prime of her life!" Sami chuckled.

"Sami, I owe you big time," Trevor said.

"Cool down, boy," Sami commanded. "We ain't got a hit yet. We just steppin' up to the bat."

Sami and Sereeta left the lunch spot early to work on a science project for the new teacher taking the place of Mr. Buckingham, who was recovering from a heart attack. The new science teacher, Lorena Walsh, was already well liked.

The three boys—Jaris, Oliver, and Trevor—remained behind with Alonee. Oliver noticed Jaris seemed troubled. "You haven't said much, dude. Don't you like Sami's idea about helping Trevor get his mom's approval?"

Jaris glanced at Trevor. Trevor knew that Jaris knew about Mr. Collier. Jaris knew the story, but he couldn't come right out and tell it to Oliver.

Trevor spoke up. "Oliver, you know what's sticking in Jaris's craw? He heard this gossip about Vanessa. Okay, my brother Tommy told me. I repeated it to Jaris, but I said I didn't believe it. The story is that Vanessa was flirting with this young teacher when she was a freshman. When he wouldn't flirt back, she got him in trouble and he was fired. Now, for one thing, she was just a kid. For another, who knows what's true?"

"How'd she get the teacher in trouble?" Oliver asked. "I mean, what's the story?"

"Tommy said she told the vice principal that Mr. Collier was flirting with her and asking for dates. So Collier got the axe."

"Oh man, that *is* bad," Oliver commented.

Trevor jumped to Vanessa's defense. "She never would have done that. Maybe this Collier really *was* flirting with her. He wouldn't be the first teacher who did something like that. It goes on a lot. I hear about it on TV. How come everybody is so ready to believe Vanessa was lying?"

Alonee had an unhappy look on her face, but she didn't say anything. She waited until lunch was over, and then she approached Trevor privately.

"Trevor, we're friends, right?" Alonee said.

"Well, sure," Trevor agreed.

"Trevor, I don't want to stick my nose in something that's not my business," she told him, "but this thing about Vanessa and Mr. Collier . . . I don't know what really happened, but I remember being in Mr. Collier's class when I was a freshman. I don't think you ever had a class with Vanessa, did you?"

"No, I didn't," he replied.

"Well," Alonee continued, "Vanessa was a big flirt. I mean, a lot of the freshman girls got crushes on teachers, especially one as cute as Mr. Collier. I had a crush on him too. But Vanessa, she'd kinda go overboard. She'd always be sitting up in front right in

90

front of him, and she'd wear these short, short skirts. Mr. Collier would look so embarrassed. I kinda felt sorry for him. He didn't know where to look. Half the time he'd be teaching to the ceiling. I'm not saying Vanessa was bad or anything. We were fifteen and we were stupid but . . ."

"Okay," Trevor conceded, "so she liked Collier. But he was a teacher. He was an adult. If he got friendly with her, it was his fault, not hers."

"Trevor, listen to me," Alonee demanded. "Mr. Collier was never accused of doing anything wrong or unprofessional. Vanessa told Mr. Hawthorne that he was flirting with her, and Mr. Hawthorne just didn't ask him back at Tubman. Now, if Mr. Collier was that kind of person, he would have lost his teaching credential, but he hasn't. He was teaching over at McKinley for years, and they took him back when Tubman didn't keep him on. All I know is, Trevor, she was coming on to him, not the other way around. You just want to be careful, Trevor. Maybe she regrets what she did. Maybe she's a much better person now. Just watch yourself."

"Okay Alonee," Trevor stated coldly, "you've said your piece. I heard you."

"Don't be mad at me, Trevor," she told him. "If I didn't care about you, I never would have said anything."

"Everybody's looking out for me," Trevor complained. "Ma, my brother Tommy, you. Everyone's out to prove that the first girl in the world who ever really liked me is some piece of trash. But I'm not buying that. You hear what I'm saying, Alonee? I know what Vanessa is and she's not what any of you think she is. Ma's wrong, Tommy's wrong, and you're wrong. Just because they never proved anything on Collier doesn't mean he probably didn't step over the line. Vanessa had to report what happened. She was protecting other girls from being harassed. So the bottom line is, I'm not giving her up, no way no how." Trevor stomped off.

Trevor's heart was pounding as he walked. The more they all tried to tear Vanessa down, the more determined he was to defend her. She was a beautiful sweet girl, and she liked Trevor. It was all he needed to know. It was all he cared about.

Trevor jogged home after school with nothing on his mind but being with Vanessa as the sun went down over the bay. Dreaming of doing that had cheered him all day. As Trevor neared the house, he saw Tommy's Mustang parked in the driveway. He was home from community college. Ma was still working and wouldn't be home until late. The coast was clear.

In a couple of hours, Trevor would be with Vanessa.

CHAPTER SIX

Trevor went in the house. "Hey Tommy, I'm home," he called. Tommy came down the hall. The brothers looked at each other. "Here, fool," Tommy snapped. He hurled the keys at Trevor with such force that they hit him in the chest, stinging him, and Trevor had to catch them as they bounced off him.

Trevor's fingers closed around the car keys. "Thanks bro," he said.

"Don't thank me, fool," Tommy warned. "If I was a decent brother I wouldn't be loaning you these car keys so you could dig yourself a deeper ditch."

Trevor went to his room to study a little, but all he could think of was that now he had the wheels to take himself to Vanessa.

Trevor drove the Cavalier to the Ice House about ten minutes before six. He didn't want to be a minute late for Vanessa. When Vanessa appeared, Trevor called out, "Hey babe!"

"Oh, you got some wheels," Vanessa noted with a grin.

"It belongs to my brother, but it'll take us down to the bay to see the sun go down," Trevor explained. "The time will be just right for that."

"Yeah, Trevor," Vanessa remarked, getting in. "You are so dope."

Trevor didn't know what she meant. He thought of himself as a dork. Kevin and Jaris and Oliver might be dope. But Trevor felt like he didn't light any fires in girls.

When they reached the beach, they hiked down a narrow little trail to the sand. Trevor held Vanessa's hand so she wouldn't slip.

"Look, the sun is already starting to go down," Vanessa pointed out. "And the sky is turning all kinds of pretty colors. It's almost like a light show."

They found a little patch of sand and sat down. It had been a warm day, but the sand was cool. Vanessa reached for Trevor's hand, and her little fingers wrapped around his. "I've never done this with anybody before," Vanessa told him. "I mean watch the sunset. That's what makes you so amazing, Trevor. Most guys would think this was so stupid. But I love it."

"Couple of times when I was hanging with my friends—we call ourselves 'the posse'—anyway, we'd come and watch the sun go down," Trevor said.

It was growing cool as the sun vanished into the horizon in a splash of scarlet. Vanessa spoke. "Trevor, my dad used to say if a sunset happened like every twenty years, thousands of people would gather to watch the spectacle. But since it happens every day, we take it for granted."

"Your dad must be a deep guy," Trevor remarked.

"Yeah," Vanessa agreed. "When I was a little girl, I thought he was the greatest man who ever lived. But then I got older and he changed." She paused and looked a little forlorn. "Or maybe *I* changed."

"He was too strict, huh, Vanessa?" Trevor asked with understanding.

"Oh man, was he ever! I felt like he had a leash on me," Vanessa said.

"I hear you," Trevor said. "My ma's like that." He collected his thoughts before going on.

"Listen, Vanessa," he started, "right now my ma doesn't know that you and I are friends, but she knows about you being a dropout and stuff. So this girl at school, one of my friends, Sami Archer, she's worked something out. Her mom is taking my ma to the Ice House for frozen yogurt on Wednesday. Sami's mom is a big, pretty lady. My ma is really tall. You gotta wait on them and be extra nice to them. Sami's mom, she's gonna say you're a nice hardworking girl, and she's gonna ask you if you're going for your GED. You gotta play along, say you're sorry you quit Tubman and stuff, and you're studying for your GED. Then maybe my mom will feel better about you and me being together, you know?"

"Okay Trevor, I'll do my best," Vanessa agreed.

"See," Trevor continued, "Ma thinks kids who drop out of school are really bad, and she wouldn't want me going around with a girl like that. But once she meets you and sees how sweet you are, and how you're going for your GED and stuff, she might soften up. I hate having to keep our friendship secret from my ma, Vanessa. I love my ma, and she's done a lot for me and my brothers. So I like to be up front with her."

"I'll be as sweet as pie, Trevor," Vanessa told him.

Trevor didn't want to spoil the beautiful afternoon by bringing up the story of Vanessa and Mr. Collier, but it nagged at him. It lurked in the back of his mind like something dark and scary, and he wanted to know the truth.

"Vanessa," he said with some hesitation, "I hate to talk about this, but some of the kids at school remember you at Tubman and they say things, stuff I can't believe."

"Uh-oh!" Vanessa said with mock horror. "I was such an awful little jerk back then."

"The thing they're talking about is this teacher, Mr. Collier," he went on. "I remember having him for history, but you weren't in that class. But they tell me something about you being mixed up in him being fired or something."

A very sad look came to Vanessa's face. Trevor expected she was going to tell him that Mr. Collier seemed nice but that he had a dark side, that he said inappropriate things to pretty girls. He did those things when he was alone with them. Trevor was ready to believe her.

"Oh Trevor, Mr. Collier was young and good looking, and I really had a crush on him," Vanessa admitted. "All the girls liked him. I was like fourteen or something. I flirted with everybody when I was fourteen, going on fifteen. My parents, you know, tried to get me in line, but I was such a little rebel. I thought I was in love with Mr. Collier. I even had a fantasy of him and me running away together. And every time he smiled in class, I thought he was smiling at *me*. I just dreamed of him and kept his picture by my bed. Then one day he asked me to stay after class. I was so excited. I thought he was going to tell me that he cared about me too in a special way."

"So what happened?" Trevor asked.

"Mr. Collier changed," she answered. "That nice, smiling, handsome teacher who I loved turned into an angry monster. He told me I was evil and wicked. He said I made him sick to his stomach. He told me I disgusted him. He said if I don't change my ways I'll have a miserable life, and I'll deserve it. He said I'd end up in juvenile hall with other bad girls if I didn't stop flirting with men like him who were older and *married*. I didn't even know he was married. Oh Trevor, I burst into tears. I was hysterical.

He didn't care. He said I should wipe my face and get out of his sight, and if I ever act like that again he'll have me thrown out of class. I never was treated so awful in all my life. I was so crushed. Then I was angry. He said such terrible things to me, and I had almost *loved* him!"

Vanessa looked down at the sand for a few seconds, then she continued. "I went to see Mr. Hawthorne, the vice principal. I was wild with rage. I told him a lot of lies. I told him Mr. Collier was trying to make dates with me, and he was harassing me. Mr. Hawthorne really freaked. I don't know if he believed me or not, but I guess he just thought it'd be safer if he didn't keep Mr. Collier at Tubman. So Mr. Collier wasn't, you know, asked back."

"Uh, did you ever tell Mr. Hawthorne that you'd lied about Mr. Collier, Vanessa?" Trevor asked.

"No," Vanessa confessed. "I thought I'd get in terrible trouble. I thought there was some law I'd broken, that telling those lies would get me sent to juvie or something.

But later on I heard his old school hired him back, so that made me feel better. I mean, I didn't ruin his whole life." Vanessa reached out and put her hand over Trevor's.

"I know it was a terrible thing I did, and I wouldn't blame you if you didn't want to see me anymore, Trevor," she told him.

"No, no," Trevor protested. "It took a lot of courage for you to tell me the truth like you just did. You could've lied, and I would have believed you. A lot of kids would have just covered it up with more lies. I really respect you, Vanessa, that you owned up to what you did. You were just fourteen, and that's a stupid age. I was about that age when I did something stupid, you know. My ma almost killed me. But that one stupid thing I did wasn't me. And what you did wasn't you. Anyway, we're older now, and we got more sense, right?" Trevor leaned over and kissed Vanessa on the cheek.

"Oh Trevor," Vanessa said, "you're amazing. I never knew there were boys out there as cute as you and as understanding."

"Well," Trevor responded, taking Vanessa's hand and pulling her to her feet, "I guess it's time we head back. I'll drop you off at your apartment."

"I'm so glad we had this talk, Trevor," Vanessa said as they went up the steep path to the street and got back in the car. "Thanks for bringing it up and just getting it in the open. Otherwise you'd be thinking about it and wondering. I want you to trust me. I want us to be honest with each other."

"Yeah," Trevor agreed and started driving.

They drove in silence for a minute or so. Then Vanessa spoke.

"Tomorrow, when Sami's mom and yours come to the Ice House, I'll try really hard to make your mom like me," Vanessa promised. "I don't remember a lot of the kids at Tubman, but I do remember Sami. We weren't friends or anything, but she had this pretty face. She was always surrounded by other kids. I envied how popular she was. She was always helping somebody out too. Whatever charity drive was going on to collect money or food or something, she'd be the chairman. And when someone was in trouble, they'd end up crying on her shoulder. That's how she was when she was a freshman."

"She's still that way," Trevor said.

"That's nice," Vanessa remarked. She kissed Trevor when they got to her apartment, and she jumped out of the car. All the way up the walk she waved to him. Trevor started the engine then and drove for home. He needed to get Tommy's Cavalier home safely and on time. It wasn't eight-thirty yet.

Ma wasn't home when Trevor walked in, and Tommy was working on his laptop. "Well, did you ask the babe about the Collier deal?" Tommy asked. "Wait, don't tell me. She said Collier was a snake in the grass, and he really came on to her. She did the right thing getting him fired. She was just a poor little freshman, and he kept jumping out of the eucalyptus trees to grab a piece of her. Is that about it?"

Trevor looked hard at his brother. "Yeah, I asked her, and she told me the truth. It was a hard thing for her to talk about, but she told me everything. She flirted with Collier and when he called her on it, she got even by ratting him out to Mr. Hawthorne with lies. She admitted she did a bad thing and she's sorry. She came clean, Tommy. But she was only fourteen when it happened, and kids do stupid things when they're fourteen."

Tommy took a long, deep breath. "Well, okay, I give her credit for leveling with you. I didn't think she had that much good in her, but I guess I was wrong."

Trevor put the car keys down on the table. "We had a great time watching the sunset. Thanks again for the wheels, Tommy."

His brother said nothing.

Trevor made an effort to tidy up the house before his mother got home. Usually the family had some sort of casserole for dinner—chicken, corn, peas, baked with cracker crumbs on the top. Trevor got everything ready to put into the oven. Then he chopped lettuce, tomato, and cucumber for the salad and stored it in the refrigerator. Ma would appreciate that. And tomorrow was wash day, so Ma would get an invitation to eat frozen yogurt with Sami's mom. Trevor hoped the visit would help Ma see Vanessa for who she truly was, a nice girl, a hardworking girl with plans to better herself, not just a high school dropout.

When Trevor got to the Tubman campus the next morning, he ran into Alonee and Oliver. The last time he spoke with Alonee, he was pretty harsh, and his behavior had bothered him. He was angry that she was coming down on Vanessa for something that was probably a lie anyway. But Trevor liked Alonee too much to be angry with her for long. He knew she was saying those things because she was concerned for him.

"You guys," Trevor announced to Alonee and Oliver, "I talked to Vanessa yesterday about Mr. Collier. I asked her what really happened." Trevor could see from the looks on their faces that they expected she had denied everything. "Vanessa admitted everything. She flirted with the teacher and then lied about him when he gave her a tongue-lashing. She feels ashamed and guilty for it. She said the only thing that helped her was when she heard he had another teaching job and was doing great. She'd feared she'd done him permanent damage, but it turned out okay."

"Well," Oliver admitted, "at least she owned up to what she did."

Alonee confessed, "I felt so bad Trevor, about some of the things I said yesterday. I was worried for you, you know. When a member of the posse seems to be getting in trouble . . ."

Trevor smiled at Alonee, "That's okay, Alonee. I always know where you're coming from, and it's always a good place."

Later that day, after school, Sami's mother called her daughter on her cell phone. She and Trevor's mother had finished their frozen yogurt treat, and all went well.

Sami hunted Trevor down. He was waiting for Tommy to pick him up. "Trev," Sami told him. "Lissen up, dude. Mama told me it went good. Mighta even been a home run for our side, baby. The girl was sweet and polite, and your mama got real quiet like this is not what she expected *at all*. When Vanessa talked about getting her GED, your mama lit up like a Christmas tree. She's even givin' the girl motherly advice, that it's not too late to make everything right in her life, that she can be forgiven, and she might just want to go home and live with her parents, 'cause she seems like a special kind of girl."

Trevor gave Sami a big hug. "Girl, you're fierce," he told her.

Trevor called Vanessa on her cell phone and told her what Sami had said.

"Oh Trevor," Vanessa told him, "I'm so glad. I tried really hard to impress your mom. Your mom seems like a really good person, but she seems really tired. It must be hard to work those long hours at the nursing home."

"Yeah," Trevor agreed, "so Vanessa, you told her you were going for your GED huh?"

"Yeah, she really liked that," Vanessa said. "She values education a lot. I told her I was really sorry I dropped out of Tubman, and I'm going to get my GED and then maybe go to community college. She told me that was good, because it's not too late for me."

Trevor paused and then said, "You *want* to get your GED, don't you Vanessa?"

"Oh wow! I never really thought about it, Trevor. I mean, could I even pass the test? I've forgotten everything and the thought of all that studying," Vanessa's voice trailed off.

"But Vanessa, you want something better than working at the Ice House, right?" Trevor prodded. "And without a high school diploma, you sort of get written off any good jobs."

"Trevor," Vanessa said, "my sister dropped out of Tubman too, and now she and Bo are making lots of money on the Internet. They're selling lots of stuff. You'd be amazed how easy it is. I'm thinking about quitting the Ice House and joining them in their business."

Trevor felt a little sad that Vanessa had no intention of getting her GED. She'd lied to his mom, but it wasn't her fault, really. Trevor put her up to it. Yet, at the time and in his heart, he thought maybe she *did* have plans for getting her GED. "What do you sell on the Internet?" he asked.

"Oh, everything," she replied. "Watches, jewelry, trinkets. You wouldn't believe how quick people are to turn over their money when they see something on the screen."

"Well, who knows," Trevor hoped, "maybe later on you'll change your mind and get your GED. You're only sixteen. You got time. Man, you could even go back to school at Tubman. Wouldn't that be great? You and me in school together."

Vanessa giggled and said, "Oh Trevor, baby, the thought of sitting in those classrooms again with all those boring teachers.

The thought of seeing Mr. Pippin again, yakking about stuff I don't care about. I don't know how you dudes stand it."

"Well anyway, Vanessa," Trevor replied, "I'm glad it went good at the Ice House, and now when I finally get the courage to break it to Ma that we're friends, maybe she won't tan my hide! I'll see you on the weekend, Vanessa, and we can do something fun, okay?"

"Oh, that'd be great," Vanessa purred. She had the sweetest voice of any girl Trevor ever knew.

Ma came home that night at ten o'clock. Trevor was in his room working on Tommy's laptop, finishing a project for Mr. Pippin in English. Ma usually just showered and collapsed into bed, but tonight she stopped at Trevor's bedroom door.

"Hey Trevor, you workin' on somethin' for school?" she asked.

"Yeah Ma, for English. I'm gonna print it in a minute," Trevor answered.

"Nicest thing happened today," Ma said. "Sami Archer's mom, Mattie, she invited me to the Ice House for some of that frozen yogurt. Tastes just as good as ice cream. Made me feel so refreshed. Mattie's such a sweet thing. No wonder she got a daughter nice as Sami."

"Yeah Ma," Trevor agreed. "Everybody loves Sami. That's why we voted her Princess of the Fair."

"Trevor, the girl who waited on us at the Ice House," Ma said in a tentative voice, "was that Vanessa Allen. I know you ain't seein' her or anything, but you were eyeballin' her when you went in there. I could see that and it bothered me. But Trevor, I'm a religious woman, and I believe in people reformin' their lives, and I'm feelin' some guilt for callin' that child those uncharitable names. She seem to be a hard workin' child, and she regrets quittin' Tubman. She says she going for her GED. I need to repent of judgin' her too harshly. But we'll see. Talk is cheap. She gonna get her GED or that just talk? Who knows? Well, goodnight Trevor. Don't be workin' too late. You need your rest."

"Goodnight Ma," Trevor said.

Trevor thought to himself that Vanessa was a delight to be with. He enjoyed all the time they spent together. And yet a part of her remained a mystery to him. He felt he knew all his friends at Tubman, even the new students like Kevin Walker and Oliver Randall. But as much as he liked Vanessa, he didn't quite know her as much as he wanted to. And *that* troubled him.

CHAPTER SEVEN

On Friday at noon, Trevor got a call from Vanessa. "I'm so lonesome for you, babe," she told him. "Why doesn't Dena pick you up at school, and we could hang out for a couple hours? She'd be waiting for you after classes in the parking lot."

Trevor had still not told his mother he was seeing Vanessa. Even after hearing that Ma had a better opinion of the girl, he lacked the courage to tell her. Trevor just continued to hope that his secret would not leak out before he could tell his mother himself.

"Sure, Vanessa, that'd be good," Trevor agreed. When he closed his cell, Jaris asked, "Your mom know yet how close you and Vanessa are getting?"

"Jare, I keep putting off telling her," Trevor admitted.

"It's your business, dude," Jaris advised, "but I think you're making a big mistake. If she finds out from somewhere else, your mom is gonna be mad. Sami said your mom seemed really friendly with Vanessa. She might surprise you by being okay with you hanging with the chick. But if she finds out you been doing it behind her back . . ."

"Yeah," Trevor agreed. "We're going to take Ma to dinner some Sunday, me and Tommy. We agreed to do that. Maybe this Sunday. When she's in a really good mood, I'll tell her. It won't be easy, but I will."

"Yeah, that's best," Jaris assured him.

"Hey Jaris, how's your little sister doing? Chelsea doing okay?" Trevor asked, trying to change the subject. He remembered Tommy saying how Chelsea had hung with a bad crowd earlier in the year and how Jaris had to rescue her or there may have been serious trouble.

"Yeah, chili pepper is fine," Jaris answered. "I'm keeping my eye on her, though."

"My brother," Trevor said, "he told me she's had some scrapes. That she was hanging with some dude from Tubman, and you had to get her out of a party where they were doing bad stuff. He said you got Chelsea out of trouble before something bad could happen."

"Yeah, that's true," Jaris admitted. "I never told anybody. I promised Chelsea I'd keep her secret as long as she stayed out of trouble. Tommy must have heard about it from someone else at the party."

"You know what Tommy said?" Trevor asked. "He said Chelsea never would have tried to sneak off to that party if she had a mom like we got. He said because your parents are easier on you guys, Chelsea felt she could do something risky. But we Jenkins kids are so scared of Ma, we'd never step over the line. That's what Tommy said."

Jaris did not respond immediately but looked a little steamed. Then he spoke. "I guess that's true. Mom and Pop, they're great parents, but they never hit us. Never. You've told me about your mom whupping you until you were sore. It's just amazing to me, dude. If anything like that happened to us, to me and Chelsea, man, I'm not sure what I would have done. The idea of getting beaten by a parent, man, it blows my mind."

"I guess when my father left, Ma went over the edge," Trevor suggested. "She thought she had to whup us into line even if we didn't need it. Maybe she was taking out her pain on us. I had a nightmare the other night. She had this knotted wet towel, and she was whacking away at my face. I could almost feel my face swelling up. I jumped out of bed and checked my face in the mirror, and I couldn't believe it was okay, the nightmare was so real."

"She whipped you with knotted wet towels for real?" Jaris asked.

"Yeah, I remember sassing her when I was fourteen and that old wet knotted towel," Trevor recalled.

Dena picked Trevor up from Tubman right after school. Dena was only twenty, but she looked much older. She looked hard. Her eyebrows were thinly plucked, and she wore a lot of eye shadow and mascara. Trevor didn't think it made her look pretty. It just made her look older and hard, like she was thirty or so.

"Hey Trevor," she greeted him. "Have a good day at the house of horrors? That's what we used to call Tubman. Me and my friends really hated school."

"It's not bad," Trevor said. "I like some of the teachers, and my friends are great."

"Does Mr. Pippin still teach English?" Dena asked.

"Yeah," Trevor replied. "Vanessa wanted to know that too."

"He still carry that old briefcase and look like he's going to his own execution?" Dena asked.

Trevor laughed. "Pretty much."

"I thought I'd die in that classroom," Dena continued. "He taught freshman English when I went there. I'd draw this grid in my notebook with a square for each five minutes of class. The only thing that kept me going was when I could darken a square every five minutes. That's how I psyched myself out and kept sane."

"Did you drop out of Tubman when you were a sophomore too, Dena?" Trevor asked her.

"Yeah. I ran away from home," Dena replied. "I hid out with friends for a long time. I came home for a while. But it didn't work."

"I bet your parents were worried, Dena," Trevor commented.

"Oh yeah," Dena said. "When I'd be gone, they were pestering the cops to look for me 'cause I had to be a kidnap victim, you know. My parents always been clueless."

"You friends with your parents now?" Trevor asked.

"Yeah, we're okay," Dena nodded yes. "They sort of gave up on me and Vanessa too. They finally faced the fact that we are what we are. Parents don't own their kids, you know. They gotta let go. I mean, if you want to own something, get a dog, right?"

They pulled up to the apartment, and Trevor heard loud music pouring out of the windows.

"That's Bo playing the drums," Dena explained. "He has this fantasy that he'll be a big rock star someday with a hot band. Like that's ever gonna happen."

"He your boyfriend, huh?" Trevor asked.

"Yeah," Dena said without much enthusiasm. Trevor didn't blame her. Bo seemed like a loser.

They went into the apartment.

"Hi babe," Vanessa cried when she saw Trevor. She threw her arms around him and gave him a big hug. "We just got pizza delivered. It's hot and fresh," she told him.

"It's the kind with pineapple on top, the really yummy kind."

Trevor settled down in one of the bean-bags and ate his slice of pizza until Bo stopped practicing with the drums. Then they all watched a medical drama on TV.

"Ma works at a nursing home and it's all drudgery," Trevor remarked. "On this stupid show they act like all the doctors and nurses do all day is fool around with each other."

Bo got up and said, "You guys, this cold is really bothering me. I run out of cough medicine. I got to get my prescription filled down at the drugstore, but I took so much medicine that I'm buzzed, you know?"

Dena looked at Trevor. "Poor Bo has had this rotten cold for a week now. He takes this strong medicine, and it says on the bottle not to drive if you took it. Could you drive him down to the drugstore, Trevor? You got a driver's license don't you?" Dena asked.

"Yeah, I got a driver's license," Trevor said.

"I'd take him myself, but I just had a couple drinks and I don't need a DUI," Dena explained.

"Sure, I can do it," Trevor agreed. Dena tossed him her car keys. Bo walked out with Trevor.

"Thanks, kid," he said.

In the car, Bo asked Trevor how old he was.

"I'm sixteen," Trevor answered.

"I'm twenty-six. I feel old already, man," Bo said. "Gruesome, huh? Ten years older than you, dude. My hair's thinnin' at the top. My legs creak when I get up. Would you believe it? Life's a piece of garbage, kid, that's what I say."

It was dark when they reached the drugstore. "You want me to go in and get your medicine?" Trevor asked.

"Nah, I gotta sign for it," Bo said. "I'll just be a coupla minutes. Don't turn off the engine. Uses more gas to start it again. Keep the engine runnin', man."

Trevor watched Bo go into the drugstore. He wore a heavy overcoat even though it was a warm evening. Trevor thought maybe he had chills from his cold.

In a few minutes, Bo came running out of the drugstore. "Go!" he yelled at Trevor. "Just get this heap movin', kid. Step on it!"

Bo seemed in a panic. Trevor heard some guy back at the drugstore screaming. Trevor went numb as he gunned the engine.

"What's going down, man?" Trevor asked as he drove. "What happened in there?"

"Don't you understand English, fool?" Bo yelled at him. "Get some speed out of this heap. I want it smokin', you hear what I'm sayin', fool?"

Trevor sped down the street, hoping there were no cops around. He kept hearing that guy back at the drugstore screaming.

What was that all about? What was Bo doing in that drugstore anyway?

Bo kept looking back. When they turned a corner, he seemed to calm down a little. He was breathing hard, and there was perspiration on his face.

"Man, what happened in there?" Trevor demanded.

"Nothin' you hear me, nothin'," Bo insisted. "Just keep driving."

Trevor pulled into the driveway of the apartment. When Bo jumped out of the car, Trevor noticed his coat pockets were bulging with stuff. Dena was in the apartment doorway when they arrived, and she asked nervously, "You okay?

"Yeah, yeah," Bo replied. He shoved past Dena, and then they both disappeared into a back bedroom. Trevor came slowly into the front room where Vanessa was still watching television.

"The guy on the show is having gall bladder trouble. Do you know what a gall bladder does, Trev?" Vanessa asked. Then she looked up and saw Trevor was soaking with perspiration and his eyes were wild. Vanessa jumped up and went over to him. "What's the matter, baby?" she asked.

"Vanessa," Trevor demanded, "what's going on here?"

"What?" she asked.

"Bo," Trevor said, "he wasn't getting any cough medicine. He ran into the drugstore wearing that big coat, and he come running out like the devil was after him. He screamed at me to get out of there fast. I saw some guy from the drugstore looking after us, screaming bloody murder. What's going on here, Vanessa?"

"Ohhh," Vanessa groaned. She walked to the back bedroom. "You guys!" she yelled. "What happened at the drugstore? Trevor's freaking!"

Dena was saying, "Oh, this is great stuff, Bo! These are fabulous. You got these too?"

"Dena, Bo," Vanessa demanded, "what's going on?"

"Nothin'," Bo answered. "Everythin's good."

Vanessa returned to the front room and made a helpless gesture to Trevor. "I wish my sister would drop that creep," she remarked. "He's nothing but trouble. Bo makes money on the Internet, but he's not worth it."

"He shoplifted, right?" Trevor stated. "That's how he gets stuff to sell on the Internet. He sells stolen goods. And I was set up. I was set up to drive the getaway car. They made me a criminal, and I didn't even know what was happening." Trevor was speaking in a bitter, emotional voice.

Vanessa reached up and lay her soft hand alongside Trevor's cheek. "Oh baby, I'm so sorry. I had no idea what they were doing. I mean, Bo has stolen stuff before, but he said he wasn't doing that anymore. I'm so sorry they got you mixed up in it."

She started to caress Trevor's cheek. He reached up and took hold of her wrist, not in a rough way, but firmly. He removed her hand from his face.

126

"There could have been trouble with the clerk. It could have turned violent, Vanessa," Trevor said to her.

"Oh no, Bo would never do violence," Vanessa protested.

"But if the clerk had confronted him, tried to stop him," Trevor persisted, "maybe Bo would have given him a push, and the clerk woulda hit his head on something and busted his skull and died. Then Bo woulda come running out, and I'm driving the getaway car away from a murder. That makes me guilty of murder too. I could be looking at a murder rap. You hear what I'm saying, Vanessa?" Trevor's voice was shaky.

Bo and Dena emerged from the back bedroom. They looked at Trevor and saw the rage on his face.

"What's the problem?" Bo asked.

"You tricked me into driving you to the drugstore, and then you jacked the place, dude. You made a criminal of me," Trevor yelled at him.

"Calm down, kid," Bo said. "Nothin' happened."

"This whole deal stinks," Trevor snapped. He glared at Vanessa. "I won't bother you anymore, Vanessa. I won't call you, and please don't call me."

"Trevor, please," Vanessa begged, starting to cry.

"Hey kid, don't freak," Bo said. "Nothin' happened."

Trevor turned and went outside. He was shaking so badly he could hardly get his cell from his pocket.

"Tommy," he said, "I hate to bother you, but could you come pick me up on Apache Street, at the corner of Grant. I need a ride bad."

"I'm on my way, dude," Tommy replied. "You okay? You sound freaked out."

"I'm okay," Trevor answered. "Thanks man."

Vanessa came outside. "Trevor, I didn't know anything about what they planned," she said. "I swear—"

Trevor turned his back to her. She admitted Bo had stolen stuff before. She knew what he was capable of. She knew the story about Bo being buzzed on cough medicine was a crock. Bo just wanted a fast getaway, and Trevor was it. He just needed some fool in the car with the engine running for when he came flying out of the store with the stolen goods. Vanessa had to know all that. Trevor finally turned to her. "Good luck to you," he said in a choked voice. "You're a pretty girl. I hope you find somebody nice, but it isn't me."

He had really cared about her. He still did, but what happened shook him to his bones. Just that quick his whole life could have been in ruins, despite all his hard work to get an education, all his hopes and dreams, and all of Ma's hopes and dreams for him. It could have been all over. When somebody died in a robbery, the guy behind the wheel of the getaway car was just as guilty as the guy who did the murder.

"Trevor," Vanessa pleaded, "please forgive me. I know I was wrong. I kinda suspected something was fishy when Bo asked you to drive the car. But I . . ." She was sobbing. "I d-don't want to lose you, babe. You're the most special thing that ever happened to me."

Tommy's Cavalier came around the corner. The brakes squealed as he stopped. Trevor couldn't believe he got there so fast.

"Let's go, man," Tommy shouted at Trevor when he saw him.

Trevor turned and ran to the car, getting in on the passenger side. Tommy took off, the wheels screeching.

"What happened?" Tommy asked.

"Bo," Trevor explained, "Vanessa's sister's boyfriend, he tricked me into driving him to the drugstore to get a cough medicine prescription filled. Then he came running out of the store with his pockets full of stolen stuff, yelling at me to drive away as quick as I could. I was driving a getaway car, man!"

"You idiot," Tommy said.

"I know," Trevor admitted.

Tommy turned on the radio for the local news as they drove. "I hope that freak didn't conk somebody over the head in that store, bro. If the creep did, then you're looking into your own grave, man." The news came on and it was all about the city's economic problems. "Well," Tommy commented, "thank God nothing really awful happened or they'd be talking about it."

"Tommy, I can't believe what just happened," Trevor said. He was still shaking.

"Lissen up, boy," Tommy scolded. "You hang with skunks, you're gonna smell bad. This bunch is no good. Vanessa's no good. They're all bums. Vanessa wouldn't hang with people like that if she had any character. She'd be home with her parents where she belongs. And she can say all she wants about being sorry about what she did to Mr. Collier. Those are crocodile tears. I don't care how much I hated a teacher. I'd never do something like that to him."

Tommy got quiet for a few seconds, then started speaking again.

"Lissen up, little brother. When it comes to protecting you from Ma, I don't have your back anymore. You do something stupid, I'm letting her know. I don't care if she whups you up one side of your head and down the other. I won't tell her anything about this, but if you screw up again, I'm on her side. You hear what I'm saying?"

"Yeah," Trevor answered. He felt sad and sick. For a little while he had a girlfriend. He thought about her many times during the day, and the thought of her made him happy. He was one of the guys, with a girlfriend. He worried about his mother's reaction, but still life was good. Now that world had all fallen apart. Tommy said it all when he bitterly called him an idiot.

"That's what I am," Trevor thought as he walked into the room he shared with his brother—a fool and an idiot. He thought he didn't even deserve a girlfriend.

Trevor showered and tried to sleep, but his cell phone kept ringing. He could see the calls were from Vanessa. He couldn't talk to her. He transferred all his incoming calls to voice mail. But he couldn't sleep anyway.

CHAPTER EIGHT

As he jogged to Tubman on Saturday morning for track practice, Trevor listened to his messages. He thought he might as well listen to them and then erase them. After a couple of hangups, she finally left a message.

"Trevor," Vanessa begged, "please call me. I'm moving away from my sister. I'm going home to my folk's house. I'm going for my GED, Trevor, honest. I told Dena I didn't want anything more to do with her as long as Bo was with her. Please call me."

There were ten more messages, all saying the same thing. "Please talk to me," Vanessa cried. "Didn't you get my other messages?" On the final message she seemed to be sobbing.

Trevor just wanted to run. He felt as if he was going to explode, and he just needed to run. He wanted to run so fast that he could clean all the thoughts of Vanessa from his brain.

Coach Curry was talking with Kevin Walker and Matson Malloy. Marko Lane had just arrived. Trevor was training for the 100-meter dash, along with Kevin, Matson, and Marko. Trevor hadn't run in this event before, but Coach Curry was impressed with his speed. He thought Trevor had a real shot to win the event in the meet against Lincoln because the Lincoln boys were not strong in the 100 meter.

Kevin, Marko, and Matson ran first, and Coach Curry timed them. All did better than their previous times. Then it was Trevor's turn. He didn't know what got into him, but he ran his own personal best time. He literally flew down the track. Coach Curry yelled, "Way to go, Trevor!"

Afterward, Kevin Walker was sitting on the bench drying the perspiration off his

face with a towel. It was a hot, muggy
morning. Kevin had recently moved to the
town from Texas, and he was living with
his grandparents. He lost his father at a
young age when the man went to prison for
murder and then died in a prison riot. Then
his mother died. Kevin tried to keep his
past a secret from his new friends at
Tubman High, but his girlfriend, Carissa
Polson, inadvertently let it out. Then Marko
Lane taunted him mercilessly about it.
Kevin almost came to blows with Marko
and would have beaten him half to death if
he hadn't stopped his rage in time.

Trevor figured Kevin would know what
he was going through. Kevin's dad was out
of his life, like Trevor's dad. The only difference was that Kevin lost his mom too,
while Trevor lived with a mother who was
often impossible. "Hey dude," Kevin said,
smiling at Trevor. "You were really on fire
out there."

"Yeah," Trevor replied. "I think I was
trying to run outta this world, you know?

Sometimes when you run, you just want to go faster and faster. like maybe you'll get to a place where you feel more comfortable."

"What's up, man?" Kevin asked. He was a nice guy. He had a bad temper, but he was getting it under control. He forgave Carissa for blowing his secret. If you gave him half a chance, he was a good friend.

"Kevin, I got a really tough Ma," Trevor explained. "She doesn't think a guy my age should have a girlfriend. I got no dad and she's trying to be mother and father. I got a girlfriend and hid it from Ma, but the girl turned out to have problems. I was really happy for a while, but now I dumped the girl. I still care about her, but I can't forgive her."

"What'd she do, man?" Kevin asked. "Cheat on you?"

"No," Trevor answered. "She has this creepy sister and the sister's boyfriend tricked me into driving a getaway car when he jacked a drugstore. He ripped off a lot of stuff, then came running out yelling at me to drive away fast. I got really scared. I thought, 'What if the jerk had hurt somebody in the store?' That would be on me too 'cause I drove the car."

"But what did your girlfriend do? Did she know about the plans?" Kevin asked.

"I don't think so," Trevor admitted. "But I think she may have suspected something was wrong."

"Maybe she's just a dippy kid who had no clue," Kevin suggested.

Trevor played Vanessa's last messages, the ones he hadn't erased, for Kevin. Kevin listened intently. He seemed to really want to understand and to help Trevor sort out the situation.

"Sounds like she's trying to turn her life around, man," Kevin commented.

"But I felt like such a fool," Trevor said.

"Tell you what, Trevor," Kevin suggested. "Call the girl. Tell her you have a lot of thinking to do. See if she means what she says. If she moves back with her parents and leaves the sister and the jerk boyfriend, then give her a chance. I was really ticked off at my girlfriend when she told her mom all about my past, stuff I was trying to hide. I wanted to blow her off too, but now I'm glad I didn't. Carissa means a lot to me now, and I'd have messed up all that if I hadn't overlooked what happened."

"You think, Kevin?" Trevor asked. For the first time since the incident happened, Trevor had a little hope. Maybe it wasn't all down the drain after all. "Thanks Kevin, thanks man."

As Trevor was jogging home, he stopped to try to get Vanessa on his cell phone.

"Hello, Trevor," she answered eagerly.

"Vanessa, look, just give me some time, okay?" he asked.

"Oh Trevor I am *so* sorry," Vanessa said. "You have every right to be angry and to hate me."

"I don't hate you," Trevor objected. "It just shocked me so much what could have happened. It's like my whole life could have been ruined."

"I know," Vanessa replied. "I never shoulda trusted Dena not to get involved in stuff like that. I shoulda stopped Bo when he asked for a ride, that dirty rat. I'm not saying it wasn't my fault too. I knew they weren't squeaky clean."

"You really moving out of the apartment and going back to live with your parents, Vanessa?" Trevor asked.

"I'm half moved already, Trevor," the girl responded. "I don't have much stuff. I travel light. My dad's gonna come and pick me up."

"Your parents okay with you coming home, huh? Like they forgave you and stuff?" Trevor asked.

"Oh yes," she said. "They deserve a better daughter than me. They've been wonderful, Trevor. They're so glad I'm coming home. It's gonna be good, Trevor. See, my big mistake was in looking up to Dena. I was the kid sister and everything she did seemed so cool, like dumping school, hanging out with creepy people who smoked dope. But I've learned my lesson."

"Well, maybe later on we can get together again, Vanessa," Trevor suggested.

"And I'll make it up to you, Trevor," Vanessa promised. "I'll get my GED, and I'll be the person you thought I was."

"Okay Vanessa," Trevor said. "Let me just have a little space. I got a track meet coming up and I want to concentrate on that. We'll talk in a couple days, okay?"

"Okay, sure," Vanessa agreed. "Just so I know you don't hate me."

"I could never hate you," Trevor said.

Trevor resumed jogging toward home. Before he got all the way there, he noticed Marko Lane coming up behind him.

"We're closing in on the Lincoln meet, huh?" Trevor said when Marko caught up, but he kept jogging. "I hope it's not hot and muggy like it is today."

Marko ignored the comment. There was a nasty grin on his face. "Hey Trevor, I know who your hot chick is. Vanessa Allen.

Girl who works with her at the Ice House gave us all the gory details. She's some chick, boy. You always were girl shy 'cause of your mean mama, but once you busted out you really went for a smokin' babe. No wonder her red lipstick was all over your face."

"Ma's not mean, just strict," Trevor corrected Marko.

"She whups you, right?" Marko said. "My mom never whupped me once."

Trevor thought to himself that maybe Mrs. Lane should have whupped Marko a few times. Then maybe he wouldn't be such a cruel jerk. Maybe he wouldn't be taunting other kids all the time or disrupting Mr. Pippin's English class. "You get away with murder, dude," Trevor told him. "Somebody shoulda reined you in a long time ago."

Marko laughed. "Nobody messes with me, not even my parents. They know better. But one time I was passing your house and you were cryin' like a little girl 'cause your ma was after you with the broom. She's big as a man and tougher than most men. I think she could whup anyone who messed with her."

"What happens in my family is none of your business, Marko," Trevor finally snapped.

"Your mama know you got a hot chick on the line, dude?" Marko asked with a taunting sneer dancing on his mouth.

"Yeah, sure she does," Trevor lied.

"I bet she don't have a clue," Marko said. "I bet if she found out her little boy was playing with a babe like Vanessa Allen, she'd get that old belt out and she'd whup you good. You wouldn't be able to sit down for a month, boy."

Trevor stopped short and turned to face Marko, who also stopped next to him. "Where're you going with this, Marko? What's this all about?"

"I'm not going to tell your mama, Trevor," Marko promised. "I don't do stuff like that to my bros. And we're friends, right? I ain't telling her how you had this chick's lipstick all over your face that night. That'd make your ma want to get an even bigger belt to whup you with. But, no, I ain't blowing your cover, dude. But since I'm not telling your mama secrets like that, I'm thinking maybe you'll do something nice for me." Marko got a glint in his eyes. The smile danced on his mouth again, like a snake writhing around his teeth.

"What are you talking about, man?" Trevor asked.

"Next week we got that meet at Lincoln," Marko started to explain. "My daddy and some of his big shot friends and business associates are coming to see his son—his *only* son—run the hundred-meter and win. Lincoln guys are weak in that event, so it'll be going to Tubman for sure. Questions is, who wins—you or me? Walker and Malloy are gonna run in another event, so it's you and me against each other and against Lincoln. My dad told all his friends I was the fastest on the team, that I'm bound for the Olympics. I wanna win the hundred-meter event, dude, simple as that. I just seen you run and you can take me out if you run as fast that day. I don't want my father disappointed. You hear what I'm saying?"

"Marko, you are one slimy jerk," Trevor told him.

"Hey dude, I'm just thinking of you, don't you see?" Marko weaseled. "I don't want to see you whupped by your big mama. Dude, she gets mad enough, she could end up killing you, maybe maiming you for life. Doing you great bodily harm."

"I've always run my best in every event I've been in, and this won't be any different," Trevor declared.

"You can run your best in the relay, man," Marko said. "You'll help Tubman win in the relay. But just ease up a bit in the hundred meters. That's all I'm asking, dude. Just don't run like you did today for Coach Curry. I never seen you run like that, and if you do it on Wednesday you're gonna beat me, most likely, and bring great sorrow and shame to the Lane family. You know what my father is gonna feel like if he's embarrassed in front of all his friends?"

"I don't care about the man and his stupid gold chains and him thinking he's better than everybody else," Trevor said.

"Don't dis my daddy, sucka," Marko warned. "My daddy's a great man. Your father is a drunk bum. He goes around begging for change so he can buy rotgut liquor."

Trevor didn't even like his own father, but Marko's words still irked him. They were low and cruel. Trevor wished he could punch the sneer off Marko's face, but Trevor was never a fighter. In all his years in school, Trevor never got into a fight. He always walked away from conflict or insults. But now he was filled with red hot rage. To hear Marko mocking his father was like pouring salt on the wound. Trevor wished he were more like Jaris, or Kevin, or Oliver, because they would take Marko on. But he wasn't.

146

Marko laughed, seeing the frustration on Trevor's face. "You wanna fight me, dude, but you ain't got the guts. You're too much of a coward. That's because your mama has beaten all the fight outta you. You're so afraid of that woman that you'd crawl over red hot coals rather than make her mad at you. You just remember that on Wednesday. When you want to fly past me on that track and make me look bad in front of my daddy, you remember how much afraid of her you are. You just think how she's gonna feel when I tell her about your smokin' babe." Marko laughed and then jogged off in another direction.

When Marko was out of sight, Trevor sat down on an old fallen tree. He put his face in his hands. He didn't know how he felt. As much as he hated to admit it, some of what Marko said was true. Ma had whipped all the fight out of him.

Trevor couldn't stand up to his own mother and say, "Ma, I love you, but you're wrong. You're wrong in trying to make me

wear a straitjacket and not experience anything of life. All that's done. I'm not gonna
be afraid of you anymore." But that was all
a fantasy. He knew he wouldn't do it.

Kevin Walker came along then, on his
way home.

"Hey Trevor, you call her?" he asked.

"Yeah, I did. I told her what you said. I
told her to give me some time," Trevor
replied.

"She okay with that?" Kevin asked.

"Yeah, she was good with it. I told her
I'd call her in a couple days," Trevor
answered.

Trevor looked at Kevin Walker. He was
a handsome, muscular boy. Trevor had a
friendly, bland face, the kind of a face that
wouldn't scare anybody. He looked like he
was about to smile most of the time. Kevin
was good looking but in a dark and moody
way. You could see something smoldering
in his eyes, and you didn't want to add any
gasoline to the fire, because you could get
burned bad. Kevin looked as if he'd never

been afraid in his life. Trevor said, "Hey Kevin, can I ask you something?"

"Sure," Kevin agreed.

"You ever been afraid, man? I mean, have a gut-choking fear?" Trevor asked.

Kevin didn't wait long to answer. "Yeah, I was scared they'd find out here at school that my father killed a man. I was afraid that everybody would turn against me if they knew that. It didn't happen. My friends were great about it. Only one I had trouble with was Marko Lane. Sometimes I think he's not even human. I think he's a slimy swamp snake, you know, a shape-shifter. Maybe he just took on the appearance of a human."

"Was that your worst fear ever, Kevin?" Trevor asked. "I mean, have you ever been afraid of a person?"

"Yeah, I've been afraid of a person," Kevin told him. "Me. I'm more afraid of me than I'm afraid of anybody else. It scares me that some day I'll lose it, and I'll do like my father did. I'll hurt somebody bad. I never want to do that."

"Kevin, I need to tell you something," Trevor said. "Today Marko, he came along and told me his father is expecting him to win the hundred meter on Wednesday. He said if I didn't throw the race, he'd tell my mom about Vanessa. I'm afraid he'll make it sound real wild, so Ma thinks we're hot and heavy, you know."

"Dude," Kevin chided him, "did you hear what Jaris said? You need to tell your mom about Vanessa right away. Come right out and tell her. And when Wednesday comes, you run like the wind. Don't let the snake win, dude. Don't let him take away your manhood. Let me tell you something, man. As soon as you show your mom strength, she's gonna back off. Right now she thinks you're weak. So she's gotta be strong. She thinks you don't have the strength to be a man. You tell her you're gonna make her proud because you're gonna be a good, strong man, only she's got to back off and let you be that man."

When Trevor got home, Tommy was listening to rap music. He never listened when Ma was around, but he liked it. "It's only talking with a beat," he told people who dissed his taste in music.

"Tommy," Trevor announced, "I got an idea. Ma was so thrilled when Jaris's mother took her to that nice breakfast. Why don't we surprise Ma this Sunday and go to church with her, then take her to a nice restaurant for lunch? Ma never gets to have any fun, and she'd really love that. We don't go to church much, Tommy, and she'd get a kick out of us hearing her sing in the praise choir. She really belts out those hymns."

Tommy grinned. "Good idea! When we go marching with her into the Holiness Awakening Church, she's gonna be so proud. Seeing her two boys sitting there—what a blast. And then we'll find a really good restaurant."

"Ma's spent her whole life eating plain old food," Trevor said. "Like that tasteless chicken and peas and corn casserole. We can find a place where the food is awesome. Like you remember how she couldn't stop talking about those French pancakes with the strawberries and whipped cream she had with Jaris's mom. She'd never even seen French pancakes before, and she's forty-five years old."

"Maybe a good Mexican restaurant," Tommy suggested.

"She likes Mexican food, but it'd be too much like those dollar burritos she gets," Trevor replied. "It has to be more special."

"There's a place over on the beach," Tommy said. "Jaris took his dad there on Father's Day. Jaris said it was really good. They serve this macadamia-crusted halibut and the roast beef is really tender and tasty. Jaris said it was the best meal they've ever had. It's called Ye Olde Boathouse."

"Yeah," Trevor said, smiling, "that sounds more like it. I *know* Ma never had macadamia-crusted halibut!"

"And Ma could look out over the bay while she's eating, and that'd be special too," Tommy added.

"It'd cost maybe around a hundred bucks for the three of us," Trevor figured, "and that includes the tip. And maybe we both could just order water. I could handle my half. I've been making money at the Chicken Shack, and I've saved some."

"Okay, Tommy agreed. "We'll surprise the daylights out of Ma on Sunday morning. Sunday morning always comes and there we are, laying like lumps in our beds while Ma is putting on her good dress for church. Ma feels bad about that. But this Sunday we'll be up and at 'em early, getting dressed up and wanting to go to church. I'll wash and wax my car, and instead of riding with the church ladies, she can drive up with her two boys. And then, as we're leaving church, and Ma is thinking she's gonna go home and make that awful casserole for us, we spring it on her about the restaurant. And we drive over to the beach and pull up at the ritzy restaurant where she's never been."

It dawned on Trevor that the last time he and Tommy, along with Junior who was home then, took their mother to a restaurant, it was to a fast-food joint for fish and chips. And that was over a year ago. *A year.*

Trevor thought that if all went well on Sunday, he might tell his mother in the afternoon about Vanessa. He would assure her it was nothing serious, just hanging out once in a while. Just friends who talk. Trevor thought the plan just might work. After the praise choir, and the macadamia-crusted halibut and the tender roast beef, the timing just might be right.

CHAPTER NINE

W hat's got into you boys?" Ma asked on Sunday morning. "Most times you sleepin' like logs, and now you gettin' all washed up. You usually dead to the world with the devil whisperin' in your ear to never mind church goin'. What're you gettin' spruced up for on a Sunday mornin'?"

"We're going to church with you, Ma," Tommy announced.

"Right," Trevor said.

"My goodness!" Ma exclaimed. "You boys ain't looked so nice since we went to Aunt Hattie's funeral last year! Pastor Bromley is gonna be so surprised. He always so delighted to see the young folks in church." There was a spring to Ma's step that Trevor rarely saw and a happy lilt to her voice. He doubted that anything he and Tommy could have done would have made her happier than accompanying her to church.

"And we're gonna ride in my car," Tommy declared. "I washed and waxed it especially for you, Ma."

"My goodness, is it Christmas or something?" Ma asked. "I been working so hard I clean forgot what day it is. It must be Christmas!"

Pastor Bromley greeted the Jenkins family warmly. Trevor and Tommy sat up front where the praise choir sang. Ma put on her beautiful blue choir robe and looked like a different person. The boys were used to seeing their mother in her faded old clothes, but now she looked queenly standing there with the other members of the choir.

After services, Mickey Jenkins remarked, "Well, this has been a lovely morning boys. Now back to the real world at home."

"No Ma," Trevor objected. "We're not done yet. We're going down to the bay and having lunch at the Ye Olde Boathouse. It's on us, Ma—me and Tommy."

"I must be dreamin'," Ma said in astonishment.

"No," Tommy told her, "we were talking, Trevor and me, and it's been too long since we took you out Ma. Me and my baby brother thought it was past time you had a nice lunch at a good place."

When they were seated in the restaurant, Mickey Jenkins looked around as if she had landed on another planet. The walls were knotty pine and richly decorated with the hull of an old ship, anchors, and treasures of the sea.

"Boys, this must be costin' you an arm and a leg," Ma fretted. "You shouldna picked such a fancy place."

"No Ma," Tommy said. "We got it all figured out. No problem."

Ma loved the macadamia-crusted halibut and the roast beef. "I never knew fish could taste so good," she raved. "It don' taste nothin' like the tuna we get in the cans."

Trevor laughed. "You're telling me, Ma," he agreed, remembering all the ugly sandwiches with the mayonnaise making the bread soggy.

Trevor had planned to break the news to this mother about Vanessa when the church services and lunch were over. He thought Ma would be in such a good mood that she'd take it better. Trevor hadn't seen her so happy in a long time.

To possibly spoil her beautiful day seemed almost wicked. So Trevor decided to let this day pass without bringing any clouds to blot out his mother's sunshine.

On the way home, Ma was more senti-mental than Trevor had seen her perhaps ever. "Y'know, boys, when I was havin' you babies, one after another, I was tellin' the Lord to give me healthy children. My own mama lost two babies under two. They were born sickly. I told the Lord if He give me healthy children, I will raise them right.

I know I ain't been perfect, but I look at you four boys . . . I mean especially on a day like today, I think of the four of you, and I'm so thankful and proud. So many of the girls I went to school with . . . they got children in prison. They got children dead of drug overdoses. I feel so blessed."

Trevor recalled the other night when he drove the getaway car. That one mistake could have destroyed everything. If it had been a robbery gone sour, all Ma's joy in her youngest son would have been forever dashed. One mistake. One small mistake.

Trevor called Vanessa when he got home. He told her about the nice day with his mother. "So how are you doing, Vanessa?" he asked her.

"I'm home, Trevor," she reported. "Dena's mad at me for leaving her with the whole rent to pay, but I don't care. I feel like this is the best thing I've done in a long time, and it's because of you. If you hadn't talked to me so strong, I wouldn't have had the courage to come home."

"I'm glad," Trevor replied. "My friends—Jaris and the gang—are planning a beach party pretty soon. All the girls will be there too. I'd like for you to meet them all. So when it gets closer, I'll call you."

"That sounds wonderful," Vanessa said. "I can't wait to see you again, Trevor."

When Trevor woke up on Wednesday morning, the first thing he thought about was the meet at Lincoln. The day before at school, Marko kept eyeballing Trevor and making silent warning signals. He'd poke Trevor in the arm with his index finger and wink as if to say, "Remember to slow down during the hundred meters, or else."

Trevor thought he could possibly run his best at the meet and still not beat Marko. Then Marko would think he'd thrown the race out of fear. Trevor hated that idea. So Trevor made up his mind to run as fast as he could, to outdo himself. He wanted to run better than he had ever run before just to prove to himself that he had the courage. It was a matter of pride.

At lunchtime, Jaris asked Trevor if he had told his mother about Vanessa yet.

"No," Trevor admitted. "We had a wonderful day with Ma on Sunday. We went to church with her, Tommy and I did, and then we took her out to eat at a nice restaurant. I was gonna tell her Sunday afternoon, but I chickened out. I didn't want to ruin that good day we gave her."

Trevor hadn't told anybody but Kevin Walker what happened on Friday night, how he drove that car for Bo. Although Kevin was eating his sandwich with the others, he didn't bring it up in front of anybody. He had that much integrity. He respected Trevor's need for confidentiality.

After classes ended, Coach Curry pulled up in his van, and the Tubman track team piled in. Kevin sat next to Trevor. Marko was in the back. Kevin leaned over to Trevor and said quietly, "Remember, don't let the snake scare you."

"I hear you," Trevor replied and nodded.

When they got to Lincoln, the stands were crowded, mainly with home team supporters, but a lot of Tubman fans were there too. Trevor couldn't help but notice Marko's father, wearing fine clothing and loaded down with gold chains, and his friends, just as dressed up with jewelry. Marko's father wore what looked like a very expensive suit, and one of his friends held a pricey camera to record Marko's triumph.

Before the meet was underway, Marko walked over to Trevor. "You know the drill, man," he whispered with a sinister smile.

Trevor said nothing.

"Don't stonewall me, dude," Marko commanded. "You'll be the sorriest boy in the county if you double cross me. Take a look at the man there in the stands—my father. We don't want him disappointed, do we?"

Kevin joined Marko and Trevor. He looked Marko in the eye and asked, "You wishing Trevor luck, dude?"

"You got no dog in this race, man," Marko snapped. "Bug off."

"The race is almost here, man," Kevin advised Trevor. "We got to focus now. No fear."

The runners got set for the 100-meter event. Trevor could hear his heart pounding. Usually when he ran he was thinking only of the race. Now he had Marko's threat on his mind too. He bitterly regretted not following Jaris's advice to talk to his mother about Vanessa. But Trevor kept pushing it off until it was finally too late.

When the runners took off at the gun, Marko grabbed an early lead. Trevor saw him from the corner of his eye. He had a powerful stride. Trevor's legs felt strange. One of the Lincoln sprinters went by too, and now Trevor was third.

Then something seemed to switch on inside Trevor's body. Suddenly everything felt right. It was like the other day during practice. Trevor passed the guy from Lincoln and then he started to overtake Marko.

He was running neck in neck with Marko, with Kevin's voice echoing in his brain, "Don't let the snake scare you."

Trevor flew over the finish line, convincingly beating Marko. It was the first 100-meter event that Trevor ever won.

Trevor's friends surged around him, high-fiving him and hugging him. Standing a few yards away was Marko, with a terrible look on his face. His eyes were fiery. His father and friends were already leaving the stands. They wouldn't stay for the rest of the events even though Marko was running in the relay too. Marko was supposed to win the 100-meter event, and that was all they cared about.

When Marko could finally get close enough to Trevor to say something, he hissed, "You'll be sorry, Jenkins. Oh man, will you be sorry."

After the track meet, Tommy drove Trevor home. "You were awesome, little brother," Tommy praised him. "I never saw you run so fast in your life. You were so smooth. You just glided along like some crazy machine, man."

Trevor couldn't think of anything else but how Ma would be when she came home at ten o'clock after getting Marko Lane's poisonous message. Marko had plenty of opportunity to reach Ma between the time the meet ended and ten at night. Trevor figured Marko could even go to the home where she worked and catch her during her coffee break. He'd do it too.

All Trevor could do was wait.

CHAPTER TEN

When Trevor heard his mother's old car come to a squeaky stop in the driveway, he clenched his fists. Trevor wasn't even going to pretend he was asleep. He would face his mother as she came in the door.

Ma came in, wearily as usual, and sat down in the first chair she saw, the one at the kitchen table.

Trevor brought her a bottle of the chocolate nutritional drink she usually had at night. "Hard day, Ma?" he asked through his dry mouth. His case of nerves had given him stabbing stomach pains.

"Yeah," Ma replied. She looked at Trevor. The look in her eyes told Trevor that she knew. "Here it comes," he thought.

Marko Lane had planted the bomb, and now it would explode, right here in the kitchen.

"When I come out for my break at three, somebody'd come to see me," Ma started to say. "Usually nobody there by the bench where we rest, but a boy was standin' there. Marko Lane. He was waitin' on me. Said he had somethin' to tell me, somethin' important. Trevor, it true you're datin' Vanessa Allen?"

For just a second or two, Trevor considered lying. He thought he might say Marko was lying. That would buy him a little time anyway. He thought he would tell his mother that Marko wanted him to throw the 100-meter race today and if he didn't, Marko promised to make trouble. But Trevor was done with being afraid.

Trevor looked at his mother and almost spit out the words he had to say.

"Yeah, Ma, I've seen her a few times. We watched a movie together, and once we sat on the beach and watched the sun go down."

"How come you never tol' me?" Ma asked. The old rage Trevor was so familiar with began to seep into her face like water filling a sponge. Her brows knit. "You oughta have tol' me, Trevor. I sacrificed a lot for you and you oughtn't to be doin' stuff behind my back. Y'hear me, boy?" Ma's voice was harsh.

"I should've told you, Ma," Trevor admitted. "I would've too, but you've made me so scared of you that I can't talk to you about anything. I can't come to you with my problems, like Jaris and Derrick go to their parents. I got to keep it all bottled up inside, and it's killing me, Ma."

Trevor was speaking in a soft, calm voice that belied his pounding heart. "Believe me, Ma, there've been lots of times I just ached to talk a problem over with you, 'cause I know you love me more than anybody, and your advice would've helped me, but I was too afraid to even bring anything up for fear you'd go ballistic on me."

"What're you sayin', boy, that I'm some ogre?" Mickey Jenkins cried.

"Ma," Trevor responded, "I love you, and you've done more for me and my brothers than probably half a dozen mothers put together, but I shouldn't have to be afraid of you like I am. I'm almost a man, Ma. I'm sixteen years old. I want to start doing the things a man does, without fearing that my ma is going to come after me with a belt. Don't you know how that makes me feel, Ma? You make me ashamed of who I am. I want to be a man, Ma, and I want you to be somebody I love and trust and can talk to."

Mickey Jenkins closed her eyes for a few seconds. She seemed to be shaking, but she steadied herself. "I been that bad, boy?" she asked in a hoarse voice.

"Sometimes," Trevor answered. "I know you did it out of love, Ma, but that doesn't make it right." Trevor walked over to the chair his mother was sitting on and knelt beside her, taking her worn, calloused hands into his smooth boy's hands. "It can't be like that anymore, Ma. I need to do what a boy does when he's almost a man. I'm responsible, Ma. I've kept all the rules. I don't do anything against the law and stuff. I respect my teachers. I respect you, Ma, and I always will, but I don't want to be afraid anymore."

A single tear ran down Mickey Jenkins' dark face. She said in a voice that was barely audible. "Baby, I been so afraid too. I'm not an educated person. I come from the backwoods, baby. When your father left me alone, I didn't think I could raise you all right. I was so afraid the streets would get you one by one. I been so afraid I couldn't be a mother and a father."

"I know, Ma," Trevor consoled her, squeezing his mother's hands gently. "Now we're both going to stop being afraid, okay?"

Trevor's mother wiped the tears away with the back of her hand. She smiled a little. "You an awfully good boy, Trevor, bless your heart. When that Marko Lane come to talk to me, he said you and that girl been doin' crazy things. I know that boy. I know in my heart that he tryin' his best to hurt you. You a good boy and he's not. I told that sucka to get off the property of the nursin' home. I told him I'd call the police on him. Then I got the broom and I run him off, Trevor. He ran so fast I thought he'd be flyin' like that old black crow in the garden pretty quick."

Trevor laughed and then he said, "Ma, we'll make a deal. We'll talk about stuff. You promise me that you won't get mad, and I promise you there won't be any big secrets, okay?"

"I'll go along with that, boy," Ma said with a twinkle in her eyes. "It gettin' harder for me to whup you anyway, boy, 'cause you gettin' so tall! 'Member now, though. You almost a man, but not yet. I'm trustin' you to do the right thing. When somethin' come up that you're not sure about, I'm trustin' you to do the right thing."

"I will, Ma," Trevor promised. "Oh, and by the way, I finally won the hundred-meter event at Lincoln today."

"Oh baby!" Ma declared, throwing her arms around Trevor and giving him a hug that took his breath away.

The forecast for Saturday was warm and muggy, the perfect kind of a day to go to the beach, swim, sit on the sand, and roast hot dogs. So on Thursday, the day after the track meet, Jaris, Sereeta, Sami, and Trevor were making the plans for a beach party. Sami's mother said she'd pick them all up in her big van at the Tubman parking lot around two in the afternoon. She'd return to the beach to get them around nine thirty and take them all home. There was room for eight kids in the van.

Jaris was going over the list. "Me and Sereeta . . . Sami and Matson . . . Oliver and Alonee. And, let's see, Kevin and Derrick can't make it. So there's you, Trevor, and . . ." Jaris looked up at Trevor, waiting for an answer.

"Vanessa. I want to invite her," Trevor announced.

"Your mom know?" Jaris asked.

Trevor grinned. "Yeah, we had a great talk. I'll tell you, dude, I owe a lot of it to you and your mom and that strawberry pancake, and Sami's mom. You guys really came through for me. You broke the ice."

Jaris smiled and the boys bumped fists.

Later that same day, in the afternoon, Trevor called Vanessa. "You know that beach party I've been talking about, Vanessa? Well, we got it planned for two on Saturday. We got a van taking us from Tubman about that time, and we can hang at the beach roasting hot dogs and whatever until nine-thirty. I'd like for you to come, Vanessa."

"Oh Trevor," Vanessa responded, "that sounds wonderful. I've just been hoping you'd call."

"How's it going with your parents, baby?" Trevor asked. He thought it must be hard to be away from home for such a long time and then be back under parental supervision. He admired Vanessa for making that change in her life.

"Good," Vanessa replied, "all good."

"You don't miss hanging out with Dena and Bo?" he asked.

"No. I'm done with them," she asserted. "Haven't seen them in a few days, ever since I left."

With the call complete, Trevor headed for Mr. Pippin's English class, and Marko Lane came along, going in the same direction. He seemed to be still enraged. "You think you got away with something, man, but I won't forget what you did to me," Marko snarled.

"You know what, Marko?" Trevor replied in a pleasant voice. "When you went and told my mother all that stuff, you did me a big favor. Because of that, Ma and me had the best talk we ever had. We got an understanding now. So thanks, Marko. I'm not afraid of Ma anymore, and she's not afraid of me going bad. It's just great. And one more thing, Marko. I'm not afraid of you, so don't waste your breath on threats, okay?"

Marko stood there staring in stunned disbelief. He couldn't think of anything to say, so he just stomped into the classroom in silence.

Trevor tried to concentrate on Mr. Pippin's class, which was focused on comedy writing, but all he could think about was Saturday. It would be so good to be with Vanessa again. Best of all, their time together could be pure joy because he would be free of the fear in the back of his mind that he was doing something against his mother's rules.

Trevor also looked forward to introducing Vanessa to all his friends. She remembered a few of them from her time at Tubman High, but they were different now. She was different. It would be like meeting each other for the first time. If Vanessa was to be Trevor's girlfriend, he wanted her to be a part of his circle of friends too.

TO BE A MAN

Early Saturday afternoon, everyone gathered at Harriet Tubman's statue, including Vanessa. She was the first to arrive. When Jaris and Sereeta came, she was already there. "You must've spent the night here," Jaris remarked, laughing.

"Yeah, I'm really looking forward to this," Vanessa replied.

"Your mom drop you off?" Jaris asked.

"Yeah," Vanessa said. "I told her this was my first chance to meet all of Trevor's friends."

When Trevor arrived, Vanessa ran up to him and hugged him. Sami's mother pulled up with the van, and everybody piled in. "We got sodas on ice in the back, you guys," Sami's mother sang out as the van pulled out of the lot. "Hot dog buns, hot dogs, mustard, mayo, pickles, whatever. You kids watch out for each other now. When anybody in the water, everybody else make sure they okay, understand? Some of you good swimmers, some maybe not so much. Sami, she swims like a fish."

"I got everybody's back, Mom," Sami assured her.

"Good girl, Sami," Mattie Archer said.

By the time they arrived at the beach, the morning clouds were gone, and the sky glowed a radiant blue. Everybody pitched in carrying the food and drinks down to the beach. All the while, Trevor could hardly take his eyes off Vanessa—she was so lovely in red shorts and a black tank top.

As the van drove away, Jaris, Matson, and Sereeta jumped into the water, followed by Sami. The four of them swam and splashed each other while Alonee, Oliver, and Trevor got the fire ring ready to roast the hot dogs.

"Look at them bobbing around in the water," Trevor pointed out. "Like a bunch of little kids. Boy, they're having a lot of fun. Later on, let's you and me go in, Vanessa."

"I bet the water's cold," Vanessa guessed. "I've had the sniffles for a couple days, so I think I'll pass."

Later, everybody sat on the big towels and ate hot dogs with pickle relish. The aroma of the roasting wieners blended with the pungent smell of the sea. Seagulls screeched overhead, and a few pelicans patrolled the waters farther out.

After the feast, Trevor and Vanessa took a walk down the beach, their hands linked. They watched the sandpipers playing in the surf. "Look how they run out when the tide goes out and then scramble back in with the wave behind them," Vanessa noted, laughing.

Vanessa picked up a piece of large kelp and playfully tossed it at Trevor, and he caught it and tossed it back. Vanessa seemed to be having a great time, but around eight o'clock she said, "I know the van isn't coming until nine-thirty, and I got a little tickle in my throat from my cold. I think I'll call Mom to pick me up now."

"Okay," Trevor agreed, a little sadly.

"I'm ready to go home now," Vanessa spoke into the cell. "I'll be at the top of the trail leading from the beach."

Vanessa gave Trevor a good-bye kiss and started quickly up the trail to the street. Trevor watched her go, wondering why she didn't want him to go with her. He suddenly had a strange feeling he couldn't quite identify. It was dark now, and he followed Vanessa up the trail at a short distance. When she got to the street, she looked back, but she didn't see him.

Then Trevor saw the car, Dena's red Toyota, with Bo leaning against it. Trevor walked the rest of the way up the trail. Before Vanessa got into the car, Trevor called to her, "I thought your mom was picking you up, Vanessa."

Vanessa looked stricken. "Uh . . . she couldn't make it. So I . . . I called Dena," she stammered.

Trevor looked at the girl for a long few seconds, painfully realizing how much he'd grown to care about her.

"You didn't go home, did you?" he accused her. "You're still with Dena and Bo. It was all . . . just lies."

Vanessa said nothing.

Trevor remembered Ma's words: "'Member now, though. You almost a man, but not yet. I'm trustin' you to do the right thing."

"Good-bye," Trevor called to Vanessa as she climbed into Dena's car. He wondered for a moment if she thought it meant good night. But he knew it meant good-bye. If she hadn't said it, he would have had to.

"I'm trustin' you to do the right thing," Ma had told him. Her words echoed in his head. He didn't do the right thing when he didn't tell Ma about seeing Vanessa. He didn't do the right thing by asking his bro to lie for him. And he didn't do the right thing by not telling the police about Bo. He was so scared of Ma, so scared of getting into trouble, so scared of telling the truth even when it was a hard thing to do.

At that moment, he realized how much was at stake. Why hadn't he reported Bo's theft to the police? He could go to jail as an accomplice if he didn't speak up! That would break Ma's heart.

Now he knew what he had to do. He was going to tell Ma about Bo and what he'd done. Together, they'd figure out the right thing to do.

That night he learned what it takes to be a man.